What was troubling Aubrey?

Zack wondered, a gentle smile on his lips.

"The night I handed the waiter the note, I was in an unsettled mood." He went on when she frowned. "I wanted distraction from my thoughts." Zack's smile curved derisively. "And your performance was certainly distracting. About halfway through your song, I began entertaining the idea of spending the night—or the entire weekend—in your bed."

Aubrey received Zack's confession with absolute silence. But, though it banished the haunting shadows, Aubrey's narrowing eyes and tightening lips informed him that she wasn't exactly thrilled with what she'd heard.

"My performance gave you the notion that I was available for the asking?"

JOAN HOHL

California Copper

Silhouette® Books

Published by Silhouette Books New York

America's Publisher of Contemporary Romance

SILHOUETTE BOOKS
300 East 42nd St., New York, N.Y. 10017

CALIFORNIA COPPER

Copyright © 1986 by Joan Hohl

All rights reserved. Except for use in any review, the reproduction or utilization of this work in whole or in part in any form by any electronic, mechanical or other means, now known or hereafter invented, including xerography, photocopying and recording, or in any information storage or retrieval system, is forbidden without the permission of the publisher, Silhouette Books, 300 E. 42nd St., New York, N.Y. 10017

ISBN: 0-373-48283-3

Published Silhouette Books 1986, 1993

All the characters in this book have no existence outside the imagination of the author and have no relation whatsoever to anyone bearing the same name or names. They are not even distantly inspired by any individual known or unknown to the author, and all incidents are pure invention.

®: Trademark used under license and registered in the United States Patent and Trademark Office and in other countries.

Printed in the U.S.A.

For Gregory Abrams:
For his charming company as guide along
the Big Sur. And for his endless patience
with three chattering romance writers.

One

*Promise me sun-spangled mornings and
moon-sprinkled nights.*
*Promise me warm, lazy afternoons and
sultry hot midnights.*
*Drench me in showers of rainbows to
wash away all my sorrows.*
*And in return I'll promise the sweetness
of all my tomorrows.*

Zack sat absolutely still, his gaze riveted on
the husky-voiced singer. The plaintive melody

aroused his emotions; the singer's beauty aroused his body.

Aubrey.

Her name tumbled through Zack's mind. *Aubrey.* Along with a professional photograph, the single name had been on the billing outside the small club. The name was beautiful, but it had been the photo that had snared Zack's attention. He'd stood on the sidewalk long minutes just staring at the large picture before entering the club on a spur-of-the-moment decision.

Now that he was entranced by both the singer and the song, the background sounds of muted conversation and clinking glasses faded, isolating Zack from the rest of the patrons inside the small room.

Aubrey was not beautiful—at least not in the accepted definition of classic beauty. She was not tall or willowy. She held no claim to perfection of features. Yet Zack was still reeling from his first glimpse of her less than thirty minutes before, when she'd burst onto the low platform stage like a minihurricane.

Every inch of her small, slender body moving to the up-tempo beat, Aubrey had electrified the restive audience with both her appearance and her husky voice.

She was like a tiny human package of dynamite. Zack was still feeling the reverberations from the explosion deep inside his body.

Aubrey was the most fragile-looking woman Zack had ever seen. Everything about her was small. She had delicate features set in a small, heart-shaped face. Under her slip-style, skimpy costume her small, obviously naked breasts swayed enticingly, yet somehow innocently. Her hips were as narrow as a young girl's. The image she presented was hardly that of the lush, sensuous woman many men fantasized about when they thought of rock singers.

Except for her hair. Aubrey's curly, thick, waist-length black mane was the silky stuff that male dreams were built on. Zack's palms and fingers itched with the desire to stroke and drive into that raven mane. In truth, Zack itched all over from the desire to stroke and drive. It was that startling desire that had compelled him to tip the waiter twenty dollars to deliver his embossed business card to her after the haunting notes of her final song had ended and she'd vanished like a wisp of smoke from the stage.

Zack had caught Aubrey's final performance of the evening. It had been nearing 2:00 a.m. when he'd given the waiter his card. The waiter had not returned to Zack's table. There had been no sign of Aubrey since she'd left the stage.

At five minutes after three, with a wry, self-derisive smile playing over his lips, Zack pushed back his chair. He walked through the cloud of blue-gray tobacco smoke, exiting the club and stepping into a cloud of whitish-gray fog which was rolling over the city from San Francisco Bay. Preoccupied with thoughts of the black-haired singer's rejection, Zack didn't notice the gleam of interest in the feminine glances that skimmed the length of his six-foot-four-inch frame and lingered hopefully on his handsome face.

Exhaustion robbing her face of what little color it normally possessed, Aubrey let herself into her small room. Automatically performing her nighttime ritual of cleansing her skin and teeth, she carefully hung her clothes up before dropping onto the narrow bed.

Only a week and a half to go. The phrase repeated inside her brain like a litany. Only a week and a half to go till she and the group she performed with finished the engagement at the San Francisco club, then she'd have three whole weeks until their next engagement in the lounge at a hotel casino in Tahoe. As founder and accepted head of the group, Aubrey had deliberately asked their manager to leave those particular three weeks free. Though neither their manager nor any one of the four other members that comprised the group knew it, Aubrey desperately needed to be by herself during those coming weeks. The grief and guilt she so very successfully concealed throughout the rest of the year always rose to overwhelming proportions at that period. And so she had to get away, be completely alone.

There she is again.

A frown drawing his white-gold eyebrows together, Zack shifted his position at the wall of windows to get a clearer view of the bluff, *his* bluff, and the woman standing on it.

Though clad in jeans and a hooded sweatshirt, the lone figure was definitely that of a female. She was standing less than a foot from the edge of the bluff, unconcerned with the brisk breeze whipping at the branches of the trees some fifteen feet behind her. And there was something about her...something that seemed to cry out to him.

Zack's frown deepened. He had first noticed her two days before, standing in the same position. She had arrived on the scene again the previous afternoon. Zack had felt that tug of "something" on both sightings. The nagging sense of familiarity had interfered with his concentration. And of course she was trespassing on his domain.

The woman's invasion didn't bother Zack particularly. Why she was there—always so still, always staring out to sea—did. Zack was aware that the view of the Pacific Ocean from the bluff was breathtaking. He could understand any person's enthrallment with it. But the woman's attitude was not one of enrapture with natural beauty. Her hunched stance gave off vibrations of suffering and loneliness.

Why was she grieving?

The twist of compassion in his chest startled Zack from speculation. Impatience scoring his handsome face, he spun away from the window. He didn't have time to play mental guessing games about solitary, lonely looking females with a penchant for trespassing onto private property, he grumbled to himself. He had work to do.

Thirty minutes later, the small copper likeness of a knight errant in the same state of incompletion as it had been before, Zack muttered a pithy expletive and strode from his workbench to the windows.

The woman was still at the edge of his bluff, only now, astonishingly, she was on her knees, gazing fixedly at the constantly changing blues of the restless ocean.

What was she doing? Zack was intrigued despite himself. And why was she doing it on her knees? he wondered. Was she praying?

The nagging sense of familiarity expanded inside. Damned odd. Lifting his shoulders in a helpless shrug he started to turn away just as a light clicked on in his mind. The woman's pose was similar to the statue, *his* statue, which was on permanent display in the courtyard.

Hmm, Zack mused. Was that the reason he was feeling the sensation that there was something vaguely familiar about her? Very likely, he decided. A tiny half smile played over his lips as he turned away, now satisfied at having solved the minor mystery.

Zack's feeling of satisfaction remained for all of twenty minutes.

"Oh, hell." Muttering the curse aloud, he trudged back to the window. The woman appeared not to have moved by as much as an inch.

How strange. Zack's eyebrows drew together again. The ground on the narrow path was uneven and strewn with small stones. Surely kneeling there had to cause discomfort, he reasoned. Yet she knelt, her gaze riveted on the crashing waves, her attitude one of unconcern for the wind that was growing stronger and tossing the tree branches frantically.

The phone rang, drawing Zack from the window and into a lengthy conversation with a young sculptor who was looking for a spot to show his work. Understanding relieved the frown on Zack's face. Settling into the cushioned rattan chair by the phone table, he listened attentively to the artist's plea.

As usually happened when Zack discussed the joyful, frustrating pursuit of creating a sculpture from clay, stone or metal, every other consideration retreated to the back of his mind. Long before the man concluded his entreaty, Zack knew he would accept his work into the small gallery that was situated on the first level of his rather unique complex.

The complex was the tangible culmination of a fifteen-year dream. Zack had monitored the construction of the four-level structure as closely as a mother fussing over her firstborn. Built into the side of a jutting, tree-covered bluff, the complex afforded a spectacular view of the Pacific coast called Big Sur.

Each level had a specific purpose. The lowest level, and the one most accessible to the winding road, was dedicated to the display of work by both famous and unknown sculptors. In the five short years since its official opening, the gallery had gained acclaim and had brought recognition to many unknown but excellent artists.

The second level contained a restaurant with soft, muted decor, subdued lighting and a breathtaking view of the coastline, where patrons of the gallery could relax over a superb meal while considering the purchase of one or several of the pieces of art offered. It was in the courtyard off the restaurant that Zack's famous, copper-covered statue of a kneeling woman worshiping the sunset was on permanent display. Though he was repeatedly offered exorbitant sums for the piece, entitled *Sunset*, Zack had steadfastly refused to part with it.

Zack's living quarters made up the entire third level of the complex. The fourth level was the smallest of all, and constructed primarily of glass. It was in this level that Zack spent the majority of his time, for it was this level that contained his workroom—at least for the smaller objects that he fashioned. The larger statues were worked on in stages, in various places.

But it was this sprawling complex that was the realization of his dream. Zack had begun working with metal before he was ten years old. By the time he was twenty he was almost used to living with the frustration of finding an outlet for his work. The dream or vision of a gallery that welcomed unknown as well as established sculptors came to Zack in his second year of college. The dream remained with him as he worked toward a degree in structural engineering, and on through the succeeding years as he gained success as an engineer and fame as a sculptor.

The years had not been easy. In his unrelenting drive to reach his goal, Zack had had little time for a personal life, much to the despair of his mother, a well-known Palm Springs hostess. Though Zack had indulged in the occasional *affaire de coeur*, he resisted his mother's every attempt at matchmaking.

And now, firmly entrenched on a bluff with a panoramic view of the Pacific Ocean, Zack knew there would be no more matrimonial machinations; his mother was dead.

His mind divided between the past and the present, Zack responded quietly to the young artist's effusive words of gratitude. After cradling the receiver, he stared into the distance, caught in the snare of memory.

His mother was dead. Zack smiled sadly. Even though some time had passed since her death, he found it hard to believe that she was gone. Although he'd loved her without question, Zack had never understood the lovely Laureen—Beaumont, then Sharp, and finally Aimsley—the giddy blond goddess who had come to California from New Orleans by way of Texas.

How did a man begin to understand a woman who, while doting on a younger daughter by her second husband and an older son by her first husband, could completely blank out all memory of that son's twin brother, whom she'd left behind with his father in Texas?

Zack shook his head despairingly. His mother, the darling airhead that she'd been, had never been able to answer any of his questions about the twin he didn't remember simply because she had not known the answers. The single bit of information she had imparted was that Zack and his twin had been identical.

A sigh lifting his broad chest, Zack settled back against the cushions. He had always felt a natural curiosity about the brother he'd not seen since the age of five. But the curiosity, mixed with a sense of loss, had been a passing thing, as his life had been full. But now he was alone. Up until two years before, his family had been a few hours drive away in the sprawling house in Palm Springs. Then, one by one, he'd lost them, beginning with Bruce Aimsley, the gentle, hard-nosed businessman Zack had both respected and loved as a father. Then had come the death of his mother. And finally, the relocation to Tahoe, Nevada, by his adored half-sister, Kit, two weeks after their mother's demise.

Zack missed his mother, missed his stepfather, but most of all he missed Kit, even though he spoke to her on the phone at regular intervals.

The curiosity about his twin had returned stronger than ever, with the absence of Zack's family. It had been that renewed curiosity that had compelled him to go to San Francisco to add a personal note to the legal notice of their mother's death that his lawyer had prepared to send his brother, Thackery Sharp.

It was in San Francisco that Zack had wandered into a club to be captivated by a singer named Aubrey.

Aubrey. Her name and face and song had haunted him for two weeks. *Aubrey.*

Shaking his head, Zack pushed himself from the rattan chair and sauntered to the window, his eyes narrowing as he caught sight of the solitary woman. He had forgotten about her, but she was still there, still kneeling, still staring out to sea.

"Well, damn," Zack muttered, swinging away from the window and striding to the door. "Enough is enough."

Descending the outside stairs silently, Zack loped along the path to the woman. She was unaware of him until he came to a halt next to her. Zack met her startled expression with a sardonic smile and a facetious comment.

"Are you aware that you're infringing on my private space?"

How utterly boring. Carefully concealing her reaction to the predictable California jargon, Aubrey stared impassively at the blond giant who was staring at her with impatience. She knew she was trespassing; she had blithely stepped over the chain looped between two trees across the path. She accepted the hand the man extended to her. As she rose she smothered a sigh.

The man was an impressive sight—if one was impressed by tall, handsome, golden-bronze humans who appeared to be the embodiment of the legendary California beach boy. Aubrey was not impressed, at least not on first glance.

On closer inspection, she noted the discrepancy in his appearance. A shock rippled through her as she gazed in wonder at the man's beautiful face. And his eyes! As his dark brown eyes met hers, the impact rocked her slight frame and Aubrey became aware of conflicting sensations. Although his face and eyes were those of a scholar, the rough texture of the hand gripping hers was that of a laborer. And the contact with that hand was sending tingles throughout her body.

"Might one ask what you're doing?"

Instantly annoyed by his dryly amused tone, Aubrey was still grateful for it, since it shattered the sense of bemusement gripping her. Disengaging her hand from his, she raked the hood of her sweatshirt back and speared her fingers into her hair.

"No, one might not." Aubrey straightened to her full height of five foot three inches. "One might ask my name, rank and serial number." She added tauntingly, "and that is all."

A spark lit eyes that had the color and depth of warm maple syrup. Despite her annoyance at his interruption, Aubrey felt a surge of response to the warmth in his eyes.

"Okay, let's have them."

Aubrey blinked. "Have what?"

"Name, rank and serial number." His teeth flashed whitely against his bronzed skin.

"Oh!" *Lord, he has the smile of an angel and the eyes of a devil,* Aubrey thought, gulping. She took a careful step back. "My name is Aubrey Mason. I'm a tourist." She gestured vaguely toward the road at the base of the bluff. "I'm staying at the Pine Inn Motel across the road." Noting his quirked brow at her backward move, Aubrey mirrored his expression by lifting her raven brows. "And you are?" she demanded coolly.

"Zackery Sharp, at your service, Ms. Mason." Bending from the waist, he gave her a sweeping bow. When he straightened, his eyes were gleaming with pure deviltry. "I own this joint." He indicated the entire bluff with a languid hand motion.

Exactly as she'd suspected, Aubrey mused, watching him warily. He was the owner of this...Zackery Sharp! She swallowed a groan. Aubrey had a flashing vision of the riveting statue of a woman she'd observed in the restaurant courtyard the afternoon before. Well, of course he was *the* Zackery Sharp, she chided herself scathingly. How many sculptors were there who owned gallery-restaurant complexes on the California coast?

Having literally grown up in the lap of luxury, Aubrey had been exposed to the arts all her life. Her father, Bryan Kline, a respected banker from a prestigious Philadelphia family of bankers, had been particularly interested in the work of metal sculptors. Bryan had purchased his first Sharp statue soon after the sculptor's work had received acclaim ten years before. Aubrey had recently celebrated her seventeenth birthday at the time.

Sheer astonishment widened her deep violet eyes as she stared up at him. He was so young, she thought absently, surely not more than thirty-five. And who ever expected a famous sculptor to look like this man who was watching her with such obvious amusement? He was much too handsome!

"Hello! Are you in there?" The "much too handsome" man bent to peer into her bemusement-clouded eyes.

Aubrey blinked, then flushed. "Oh! Yes. I'm sorry." She smiled tentatively. "I was trying to equate the actual man with the legend," she explained.

"Ah," he murmured in satisfaction. "You're familiar with my work?"

"Familiar!" Aubrey exclaimed around a soft burst of laughter. "Familiar hardly describes it! I've been listening to my father rave about your work for ten years."

Oddly, the sound of her laughter brought a dramatic change to his expression. His eyes narrowed, then widened, as if with sudden comprehension.

"Aubrey!"

Aubrey frowned at the note of discovery in his voice. "Yes?" She lifted one delicately arched eyebrow in question.

"The singer," Zack muttered under his breath. Then, almost accusingly, he went on, "I saw you perform in San Francisco a few weeks ago." His dark gaze swept her jean-and-sweatshirt-clad form, then studied her face free of the stage makeup. "I *knew* there was something about you!"

Aubrey wasn't sure if she ought to feel flattered or insulted by his smug expression. "Something about me?" she repeated in the icy tone of hauteur she regularly employed to discourage overzealous admirers.

"Umm." Zack nodded. "I've been watching you for some time from my workroom window." He gestured toward the house behind him with a sharp movement of his head. "And there was just something so very familiar about you." He smiled dryly. "At first I thought it was the similarity between your kneeling position and the statue in the restaurant courtyard," he explained. "But even after I'd decided that was it, I still felt the tug of familiarity." He bestowed his excitingly heaven-sent smile on her. "With the sound of your laughter, I could see you at that club."

Aubrey still wasn't quite sure whether she should feel complimented or affronted; there was an odd underlying meaning in his tone that she couldn't quite identify.

"And did you enjoy the performance?" she asked probingly.

"Oh, certainly." Zack waved his hand dismissively. "The group is very good." His lips curved sardonically. "But even though I enjoyed the music, I had, ah, other things on my mind. I paid a waiter to deliver a note to you."

Aubrey was hard put not to groan in disappointment. For some unknown reason, she had expected him to be different from the run-of-the-mill backstage Romeos.

"I never accept invitations from the customers, whether verbal or written," she replied coolly. "The waiters take the money, but they destroy the notes."

Zack shrugged. "Oh, well, you win a few, you lose a lot."

Now Aubrey definitely felt insulted; he couldn't have been all that smitten by either her appearance or her voice! But before she could think of a suitably dampening retort, he grinned engagingly and extended his hand to her.

"C'mon, I'll buy you a drink in the restaurant." His gaze swept her wildly blowing hair. "The wind's rising. I suggest we get out of it."

Until he'd mentioned it, Aubrey had only been vaguely conscious of the stiff breeze. Piqued by his overly casual attitude, she ignored the black strands whipping crazily around her shoulders and into her face. How dare the man dismiss her then offer to buy her a drink? she thought irritably, momentarily forgetting her own usual disinterest in all men. Deliberately avoiding his hand, she raised her black lash-shadowed eyes to his.

"No, thank you," she murmured with stinging politeness. "I think I'll return to the motel." As she moved to turn away, his hand curled around her upper arm. As a means of halting her, it was very effective. It was very effective in stirring her anger, too. Lifting her chin, Aubrey stared at him down the length of her short, straight nose. "If you don't mind, Mr. Sharp?" She slowly shifted her glance from his eyes to his hand then back to his eyes.

He released her at once but, strangely, his dark gaze kept her anchored to the path. "Why would you want to go to an empty motel room?" Even before he'd finished asking the question his expression changed to dry speculation. "Or isn't the room empty?"

Aubrey stiffened perceptively. "Although it is certainly none of your business, the room is empty." Aubrey used her coldest, drop-dead tone. "I am simply not looking for male companionship." She allowed a chiding smile to curve her soft lips. "Not even if the male happens to be the famous Zackery Sharp."

"Your father would never forgive you," Zack rejoined outrageously. "And the name's Zack," he added warmly, coaxingly.

"Whatever." Aubrey's shrug of carelessness came off rather well, considering the havoc his melting gaze was creating in her nervous system. Lord! she marveled, the man had enough sex appeal for an army platoon! Unused to reacting so strongly to any member of the opposite sex, Aubrey hesitated, and was thus lost.

"Please, Aubrey, join me for a drink." As if he sensed her weakening resistance and quickening interest, Zack zapped her with the full power of his devastating smile. "Please?"

"Mr. Sharp—" Aubrey began in sharp protest, the starch draining from her spine.

"Zack," he cut her off softly. "And may I call you Aubrey?" he asked, not unlike a well-behaved boy.

Even though Aubrey was positive Zack was no more well behaved than he was a boy, she slid her palm into the hand he continued to hold out to her, and immediately wished she hadn't. Though his skin was cool, it made hers feel suddenly very hot. As she followed his lead along the narrow path a frown of consternation drew a groove above the bridge of her nose.

She had not responded to a man in over three years. Why was she now reacting so strongly to this particular man? Attempting—and failing—to deny the tingle of awareness that scurried in hot waves from her hand to the nape of her neck, Aubrey trailed in Zack's wake, along the path that ran around the four-story structure to a seven-foot-high gate that opened onto the restaurant courtyard. She raised a mocking brow at Zack as he refastened the gate latch.

"I take it the path is verboten to the general public?"

"You take it correctly." Zack grinned. "The customers have the freedom to use the path that runs along the bluff on this side, which, by the way, has a rail for their protection. The open side of the bluff is mine."

"And you don't share what you consider personally yours?" Aubrey gibed softly, quickening her pace to keep up with his long-legged stride.

"I'm selective," Zack retorted, slanting a glittering glance at her. "But by and large you're right. I have a tendency to guard what I consider mine."

Aubrey's heartbeat slowed, then kicked into high gear. Had it been her imagination or had there been a hint of warning possessiveness in Zack's lowered, sensual tone? Thrown off balance, she nearly walked into him when he

paused to allow her to precede him into the
restaurant.

Ridiculous! Aubrey decided, sweeping by
him into the open, airy room and following the
maître 'd to a table for two. Why should she
imagine he was feeling at all possessive about
her? She had met the man mere minutes ago!
But then how did she explain the unusual sexual attraction humming like a live wire between them?

Wary, unprepared for any emotional
trauma, Aubrey shied away from her silent
questions by concentrating on the spectacular
view through the wide windows that ran the
length of the room. Beyond the bluff, the
coastline could be seen for miles. The blue Pacific waves crashed onto the beach and clus-
tered rocks, spraying into sun-spangled drops
of water that shimmered brightly in the clear
air.

"It's all so incredibly beautiful," she murmured in an awed tone. "Words are barely
adequate to describe it."

"Yes."

A roughness to his lowered tone made Aubrey glance up. She discovered his gaze fas-

tened to her face and not the scenic beauty in the distance. Warmed by his obvious appreciation of her looks, Aubrey felt a flush spread over her cheeks.

"I—I wish you wouldn't look at me like that!" she exclaimed in a muffled protest.

"Why?" Zack's heated brown eyes darkened to the shade of brown sugar. "You're exceptionally lovely, and I enjoy looking at you."

"You're embarrassing me." Aubrey glanced around at the other patrons in the restaurant, sighing her relief at the evidence of their obvious disinterest. "Suppose someone notices."

"Notices what?" Even as he voiced the query his gaze caressed her trembling lips.

Without thinking, Aubrey skimmed her tongue over her suddenly parched lips, gulping as his hot gaze followed the motion. "Zack, stop it!" she pleaded. "You're as much as making love to me in full view of the customers!"

"I know," Zack murmured implacably.

Aubrey could barely breathe; his words sent a combined rush of fear and excitement to her senses. "Wh-what are you saying?" She expelled her breath in a whispered whoosh.

"I had entertained the idea of spending the night in your bed."

Two

"Wh-what?"

Zack cursed himself silently for the carelessly tossed off remark; it had replaced the sparkle of interest in Aubrey's eyes with the haunting shadows he'd noticed on the bluff, darkening them to deep purple. What was troubling this gorgeous creature? Zack wondered, a gentle smile on his lips.

"The night I handed the waiter the note," he explained, reaching across the table to slide his work-roughened hand over her fingers, stilling their restless movements, "I was in an unsettled mood." He went on when she frowned, "I wanted distraction from my thoughts." Zack's smile curved derisively. "And your performance was certainly distracting. About halfway through your song, I began entertaining the idea of spending the night—or the entire weekend—in your bed."

Zack's confession was received with absolute silence. But though it banished the haunting shadows, Aubrey's narrowing eyes and tightening lips informed him that she wasn't exactly thrilled with what she'd heard.

"My performance gave you the notion that I was available for the asking?" Her delicately arched, raven brows rose disdainfully.

You stupid ass! Zack clamped his lips together to contain the self-condemnation. His nostrils flared slightly as he drew in a calming breath.

"Not at all." Zack was forced to bite out the denial through clenched teeth. "My arrogance gave me the notion that I could beguile you into spending some time with me."

Her action coolly calculated, Aubrey slipped her hand from beneath his. "I see," she murmured, sliding her chair away from the table. "Now, if you'll excuse me—" Her icy tone left

Zack without doubt that she didn't give a damn whether or not he'd excuse her. He was raking his mind for a plea that would halt her flight from the table when the arrival of the waitress made Aubrey pause before rising.

Tamping down the urge to jump up and hug the middle-aged woman who'd been with him since he'd opened the restaurant, Zack contented himself with bestowing a heartwarming smile.

"Afternoon, Zack." The woman returned the smile. "What can I get you?" She eased around to include Aubrey.

"Nothing for me, thanks—" Aubrey began.

"Coffee for both of us," Zack interrupted her.

Although anger flared in Aubrey's eyes, she remained seated until the waitress walked away. "You had no right to do that," she said with controlled softness.

"I know," Zack admitted blandly, shrugging. "But I..."

"But you're accustomed to getting your own way," Aubrey finished for him. Her angry gaze speared into his conscience and his heart. "Are you also accustomed to getting any

woman you take a fancy to into your bed?"
she demanded grittily.

"No, of course not." Zack's flat denial was
a blatant lie; in truth he *had* bedded every
woman he'd ever taken a fancy to. But he had
long since outgrown the need to prove himself
or anything else with his sexual prowess. At
thirty-five, Zack was very selective.

"I think you're lying through your teeth,
Mr. Sharp," Aubrey murmured, smiling at the
waitress as she delivered the two steaming
mugs of coffee to the table. "I'd hazard a
guess that you've been spoiled rotten by the
fame and wealth your undeniable talent has
brought you," she went on mildly after the
waitress moved away.

"Perhaps." Zack cradled the mug in his
broad hands as he murmured the noncommit-
tal response. He really didn't believe that he
had been spoiled, but he was more than willing to agree with her as long as it kept her
seated across from him. "You have an equal
talent, if in a different art form," he complimented her as he took a careful sip of the hot
brew. "Are *you* spoiled, as well?"

Aubrey acknowledged his compliment with
a brief smile, and his question with a negative

shake of her head. "As I haven't achieved even a portion of the fame you have," she pointed out chidingly, "there has been little opportunity to become spoiled."

Very slowly, very deliberately, Zack examined each of her facial features, arching one white-gold eyebrow in appreciation of the dusky rose flush that relieved the paleness of her cheeks at his perusal.

"Talent aside, I'd hazard a guess that you could have easily been spoiled for your beauty alone."

"The same could be said about you." Aubrey mirrored the movement of his eyes, her gaze sketching his features slowly.

Zack's nerves grew taut with heightened awareness. Tension simmered like a living thing in the air separating them. Zack was neither blind nor stupid; he knew the face he confronted in the mirror every morning was more than passably attractive. Yet for some odd reason, hearing this particular woman refer to his male beauty excited him beyond comprehension. Suddenly his body was hurting with a demand for intimate knowledge of hers. He tried to impose control on the hunger which coursed through him with a tongue of fire. Raising the mug to his lips, Zack inhaled the rich aroma of the brew before swallowing deeply. The liquid was unequal to his suddenly raging thirst. Making no attempt to conceal his desire, Zack pierced the depths of her violet eyes with his passion-darkened gaze.

The flame inside his eyes leaped higher with the breathless "Oh" that whispered through her slightly parted lips. Zack knew that the hunger clawing at him was blazing from his eyes, for Aubrey or anyone else to see. He also knew the restaurant was not the place to reveal that hunger. Reluctantly, he released the visual hold on her by lowering his gaze to the tabletop.

"I—I must leave now."

Zack's glance shot back to her. Every trace of color had drained from her face, and that haunted look was back in her shadowed violet eyes. The sight of her pale face and trembling lips caused a shaft of pain in his chest that was shocking.

"Aubrey." The hoarse sound of his own voice made Zack pause. His chest felt tight, his breathing constricted. *What the hell!* The confused exclamation rang inside his head. Never had he reacted to a woman like this!

Zack didn't like the way he was feeling. Nevertheless, he knew he had to see her again. He opened his mouth to deliver a suave, smooth invitation for dinner. What burst from his throat was a starkly blurted "Have dinner with me."

"No." Aubrey shook her head sharply. "I can't, not tonight." Her voice was strained, her slender body taut as she pushed her chair back and stood up. "Not tonight," she repeated in a whispered moan. Averting her eyes, she turned and rushed from the restaurant.

Stunned by her precipitous departure, Zack sat absolutely still for an instant, then he was up and moving, his long legs striding with unusual grace for such a tall man. He caught up with her as she was passing the gleaming copper statue in the courtyard.

"Aubrey, wait!" Reaching out, he curled his fingers around her upper arm, turning her to face him as he ended her flight. "May I see you tomorrow?" His throat tightened at the sight of the pain reflected in her eyes.

"I—I don't . . ." she choked.

"For breakfast?" Zack inserted when she paused. "Lunch? Dinner? *Any*thing!"

Though amazed at the pleading sound of his voice, Zack continued, "Please, Aubrey."

She shook her head distractedly. Then her glance was caught, riveted by the statue that was blazing like a red-gold flame in the afternoon sunlight.

"How very beautiful she is," she murmured, more to herself than to him.

Zack felt almost humbled by the whispered praise. The sensation was extraordinary, simply because it was completely new to him. Praise or criticism of his work had never affected him—whether it came from an expert or an amateur. The sensation was even more unusual when coupled with this particular piece of work. Zack *knew* his kneeling sun worshiper was beautiful; her very beauty had been the reason he'd refused to part with her, despite the numerous offers he had received. And yet he stood humbled before this woman's praise.

"You remind me of her." Damn! Zack winced. He had not intended to tell her that.

"I do?" A frown drew Aubrey's brows together as she shifted her glance to him, then to the statue, then back to him again.

Zack raised one shoulder in a half shrug. "I probably saw the resemblance because you were kneeling on the bluff." The explanation was the truth, as far as it went. But since Zack had never acknowledged the emotion he felt for the inanimate object, he could hardly express it to the living woman who now seemed to personify the statue. And though there was a glimmer of understanding within him, Zack chose not to examine it at that particular moment. Later maybe, he promised himself, narrowing his gaze on her deepening frown.

"I assure you I was not worshiping the sun," Aubrey responded at length, turning back to stare at the gleaming statue.

"Then what were you doing?"

"That's none of your business!" Her black mane swirled about her head and shoulders like a billowing curtain as Aubrey whipped around to glare at him in challenge. "Just because I happened to wander onto your bluff does not give you the right to pry into my life!"

"Pry into your life?" Zack repeated, stunned. "I asked a simple question. I'd hardly call that prying." He met her challenging gaze directly. "And as you've admitted, you were trespassing. Naturally I'd be curious."

"Yes, naturally." The spark of fire in her eyes was extinguished. "I'm sorry." A tentative smile tugged at her lips. "I overreacted."

The shadows were back to haunt her beautiful violet eyes. An urge to protect her swamped Zack, stunning him more than her accusation had. She looked so fragile, so lost, so very alone. Yet instinct warned him that should he offer her protection, or even compassion, she would either run from him or verbally attack.

"Aubrey?" His voice was soft, a balm to whatever was abrading her emotions. Her smile acknowledged the question contained within her murmured name.

"I'm all right." Her shoulders moved in a helpless gesture. "At least most of the time," she amended self-deprecatingly. "Please, don't concern yourself."

Her advice came too late; Zack was already concerned, and intensely intrigued by the aura of mystery surrounding her. Denying a sudden need to touch her, he jammed his hands into the pockets of his jeans. "May I walk back to the motel with you?" Zack managed to keep his tone free of inflection by sheer will power, then held his breath while waiting for her response.

Feeling herself stiffen, Aubrey made a conscious effort to relax. With firm resolve she opened her mouth to say no.

"If you like." Her eyes widened briefly in surprise at her acceptance of his offer. What was she doing? she wondered, attempting a shrug. She didn't want his or anyone's company—did she?

As she turned toward the path, she slid a sidelong glance at him. Her breath caught at the sight of him in the sunlight. He was all blond and gold and handsome, and much too charming for her peace of mind. Concentrating on breathing evenly, she swung away from him, then stopped dead when he caught her hand in his. Startled by the warmth that spread from his palm to her entire body, Aubrey raised her eyes to his.

"The path's uneven," Zack explained, stepping around her. "I'll lead the way." Tugging gently on her hand, he sauntered off. Aubrey had little choice but to follow him.

The path *was* uneven. Picking her way carefully, Aubrey descended to the short flight of stone steps where the path branched off, one section continuing down to the road, another curving around to the gallery entrance.

"It's unique," she said. "One of a kind, isn't it?"

Zack stopped and glanced at her over his shoulder. "The gallery?" He arched his white-gold brows in question.

"The entire complex." Aubrey moved her hand in a sweeping arc. "The concept. I don't know of any other quite like it."

A smile of deep satisfaction curved Zack's lips. "Yes, I know. I planned it that way."

Aubrey couldn't help responding to the warmth of his smile. "But the gallery is particularly unique. Did you plan that, as well?"

"The concept of the gallery came first." Still clasping her hand, Zack turned to look at the lowest level of the structure. His gaze was soft, dreamlike. "It was a long-held idea." His smile grew reminiscent. "Or more accurately, ideal," he corrected himself.

Even as he was making the admission, Zack was wondering why he was doing so. He had never told another person about his dreams or desires, not even his beloved sister. Yet here he was, opening up to a woman he'd just met, but somehow felt he'd known forever. It was strange and confusing, but—Zack mentally shook his head in wonder—it was also comfortable and comforting.

"You felt compelled to create a showcase for unrecognized talent?" Aubrey probed gently, her interest caught against her will.

Zack shifted his gaze to her; his brown eyes sparkled with genuine amusement. "Compelled? You mean, as in offering a helping hand in gratitude and repayment for my own success?"

Fascinated by the way his heavenly eyes could suddenly gleam so devilishly, Aubrey nodded in answer. The gleam in his eyes flared to a laughing glow.

"Not at all." Zack's tone held more than a hint of arrogance. "I feel no sense of indebtedness, no urge to pave the way for others. I've earned every advantage I now enjoy."

Aubrey was thoroughly captured. Oh, Zack was arrogant, and an individual from his toenails to the white-gold hair on his head, but he was also much, much more. The "more" cried out for investigation; something inside Aubrey suddenly yearned for explanations. Not quite sure where to begin the intriguing task of peeling layers from a man, she stared at him in consternation. Zack's bark of delighted laughter shattered her bemusement.

"Don't let my less than humble attitude throw you. I'm not such a bad guy when you get to know me." Zack's tone left no doubt in her mind that he was not offering an apology but an invitation.

Unaware that she was stepping out of the protective shell she'd lived in for three years, Aubrey accepted his immodestly issued invitation.

"And how does one go about getting to know Zackery Sharp?" Aubrey tilted her head and smiled quizzically.

Zack was on the point of replying, One could begin by having dinner with him, when he remembered her reaction to his earlier offer of dinner. There was something about this particular day that bothered her, brought haunting shadows to her eyes. Cautioning himself against blundering in where angels feared to tread, he tamped down his desire to spend the evening with her, opting instead for a fresh start on a new morning.

"One could begin right there." Zack gestured toward the gallery with his free hand.

"Immediately after having breakfast with the famous sculptor there." His hand moved to indicate the restaurant.

It wasn't until after she'd been politely escorted to her motel and was alone in the adequate-sized, functional room that Aubrey realized she'd forgotten the past, her grief and guilt and virtually everything else during the half hour or so that she and Zack had paused on the path.

"Oh, darling, I'm sorry."

The anguished whisper shimmered on the still air in the room; hot tears shimmered on the edge of her long black lashes. How could she have forgotten for even a moment? Aubrey chastised herself, sinking into a chair. An image of the beloved face rose in her mind, detailed to the last precious feature. A shudder shaking her slight frame, she buried her face in her trembling hands.

"Oh, darling, I haven't forgotten. Mommy could never forget."

Racking sobs were torn from her aching throat, finally relieving the tightness in her chest that she'd awakened with that morning.

Crouched as if in intense physical pain, Aubrey stumbled to the bed to curl into a tight

ball of misery. The flow of hot tears released
the floodgates of memory. In her mind she was
back on that little-known, nondescript island
in the Caribbean, reliving the two weeks prior
to the freak storm responsible for the accident
that had robbed her of her husband and baby
daughter.

Aubrey was positive she would forever hear
the echo of her own and her husband Keith's
raised voices on that balmy September day two
weeks before the storm. Their argument had
been the death knell to their marriage.

"I forbid you to parade around half-naked
for a bunch of drunken tourists!" Keith's angry voice had reverberated in the confines of
the small sleeping cabin that had served as
their bedroom for six long months.

"I do not parade around half-naked!" Aubrey had shouted back. "My costume is less
revealing than my bikini, for heaven's sake.
And we need the money." Aubrey had attempted reason.

"We've managed so far. You've never gone
hungry." His pride stung, Keith retaliated un-
reasonably. "I'd rather see you starve than go
back to singing."

"And what about Connie? Would you rather see our baby starve, too?"

Keith had the grace to flush. "Connie isn't going to starve. The check from my parents should arrive soon." His eyes darkened accusingly. "And if you'd write to your parents, our financial problems would be over."

Should she have written to her parents? The question had been one of the ghosts haunting her for three long years.

The racking sobs took their toll on Aubrey's stomach. Gagging, she clamped her hand over her mouth and dashed for the connecting bathroom. As she had eaten nothing solid all day there was nothing to eject but the coffee she'd drunk in the restaurant. It left a bitter, burning sensation in her throat, but the sobs ceased with the purging.

Exhausted, Aubrey dragged her depleted body back to the bed. Lying on her back, she stared at the ceiling through gritty, stinging eyes.

Had she ever loved Keith, *really* loved him? No, she had not. Sighing, Aubrey blinked against a fresh surge of tears. She had loved him as a brother, as a friend, as the next-door neighbor she'd known forever. She had not been *in* love with him. Their parents had always been close, and they were in favor of the marriage. She had never met anyone else that she'd liked better than Keith, and she'd allowed herself to drift into marriage with him. By doing so she had cheated him, and herself.

But most of all she had cheated her daughter.

Oblivious to the tears that ran in a scalding stream down her temples to soak the silky strands of her hair, Aubrey accepted the shame and guilt as her due. She had known the marriage was a mistake before their first month together was over, several months before she'd become pregnant. She should have ended it at once.

But she had tried to end it. Aubrey shook her head to deny the inner cry of self-defense. Trying was unacceptable as an excuse; she should have *done* it. Instead, she had caved in to Keith's pleas and his growing emotional dependence on her.

Fully aware of her error, she had remained with him, supporting him both emotionally and financially while he chased the dream of being a famous artist—someday. Fortunately, the manager of the small bistro she was singing in at the time allowed her to stay until mere days before her daughter, Constance, was born. After Connie's arrival, they survived mainly on the largess of Keith's parents.

In fact, it had been Keith's parents who provided the sailboat when he expressed a desire to seek inspiration by sailing to the Caribbean. Indulgent to the whims of their only child, the Masons had convinced themselves that their budding genius could indeed capture elusive fame by mimicking a Gauguin style of living and painting.

A sad smile curved Aubrey's trembling lips. Even she had hoped Keith would be so inspired by the lush islands that he'd produce marketable work. Conversely, Keith had worked less and less at painting and more and more at seeking "inspiration" by testing and tasting the fruits, and the women, of his new-found paradise. Although all intimate aspects of their marriage had ceased by the time he embarked on a course of dissipation, Aubrey could not deny a feeling of betrayal. It was then that she'd decided to find a way to take Connie and return to the States.

Why hadn't she sought from her parents the financial assistance that would have allowed her to leave the islands, and Keith, immediately?

Aubrey moved restlessly on the bed. The charge was yet another of the ghosts that continued to haunt her. She had faced the one-word answer long ago: *pride*. Her own stiff-necked pride had demanded she stay with Keith on the sailboat until she'd earned the money to pay for their flight tickets. Subsequently, she'd applied for the job of lounge singer in response to an advertisement by the manager of a relatively new hotel on the island.

Telling Keith that she had been hired as a singer had caused the argument that continued to rage in her memory.

"I forbid you to parade around half-naked for a bunch of drunken tourists!"

Aubrey was certain she'd hear Keith's angry voice until the day she died. She was as certain she'd hear her own cold tones as she flung her defiant response at him and stormed out of the cabin.

"You're not in a position to forbid me to do anything. And, since you are incapable of putting food on the table, I will have to do it."

Aubrey had slept in the boat's small lounge after that. She had started working for the hotel the very next day. Fortunately, or as it turned out, unfortunately, Keith had not balked at having to baby-sit for most afternoons and into the early hours of the evenings on the weekends. Aubrey had never questioned Keith's love for his daughter. But she later realized that she should have questioned the depths of his emotional instability.

And that was another of the ghosts that continued to haunt her.

Missing her tiny, beautiful daughter terribly, yet set on her course of action, Aubrey reluctantly left Connie in Keith's care most afternoons to rehearse with the small combo at the hotel. Even more reluctantly, she also had to relinquish the enjoyment of the bedtime ritual of bath and story book reading she'd instigated with Connie just prior to the child's second birthday.

The salary Aubrey was paid for her work had indeed put food on their table. It also enabled her to buy a few articles of sorely needed clothes for her growing child. However, the majority of the money Aubrey earned went into a savings account she'd opened for the purpose of purchasing airline tickets off the island for her daughter and herself.

Avoiding Keith as much as possible, and responding only to conversation connected to Connie, Aubrey deliberately allowed the rift between her and Keith to widen into a chasm.

Mere hours before the storm struck, the weather appeared as cloudless and calm as any other day. After making a game of coaxing Connie to eat her lunch, Aubrey left the sailboat to go to the hotel for rehearsal. Within the confines of the lounge, she and the other members of the group were unaware of the rapid approach of the tempest. By the time they were informed, it was too late to risk getting back to the boat, which was berthed at the marina on the far side of the island. Even then Aubrey had not known that the marina lay directly in the path of the swiftly spawned, wildly erratic storm.

Reassuring herself with the thought that Keith must have taken Connie and joined the rest of the island's residents in seeking shelter, Aubrey had nervously waited out the relatively short period of time in which the high winds and rain vented their fury on the island.

Less than an hour after the storm had moved on, the winds subsided to a caressing breeze and the sky was as clear as if a mass of rolling black clouds had never obscured the brilliant sapphire blue sky.

Leaving the hotel, Aubrey had run all the way to the other side of the island in search of her family. There had been no sign of Keith and Connie in the sparse crowd as the islanders and tourists began wending their way back to the dock. There was no sign of the sailboat when Aubrey breathlessly arrived at the slip where it had been berthed for six months.

Frantic with concern, Aubrey had panicked; the panic endured throughout the three days that crept by before the authorities found the wrecked sailboat and the bodies of its passengers.

An anguished moan shattered the stillness of the night. Oblivious to the sound of pain, Aubrey closed her eyes against a hot surge of tears. If she could only get through the night this anniversary would be over—this hated anniversary of the day she'd lost her beautiful little girl.

Three

____

It was a beautiful morning. His pajama pants riding low on his hips as he stretched languorously near the wall of windows in his bedroom, Zack raked long fingers through his tousled hair and fixed his gaze on the face of the bedside clock. The hands made a straight line between the twelve and the six.

Was it too early to wander across the road to Aubrey's motel? Zack grimaced. Yes, of course it was.

After he'd spent the evening and most of the night in anticipation, the idea of waiting even one more hour to see her seemed intolerable.

Strange, he had never itched quite this badly for the company of a woman.

Shaking his head, Zack turned away from the swirling pinks, blues and mauves of the dawning morning. At any other time the natural beauty would have arrested his attention. Not so this morning; this morning Zack had more important things on his mind.

Even getting dressed took on an importance that was out of proportion. Baffled by his own indecisiveness, Zack raked through the clothes closet that ran the entire length of one wall, selecting then discarding one group of slacks and shirts after the other.

"This is crazy!"

With the exasperated exclamation, Zack flung a pair of lightweight brown slacks and a pale blue knit pullover onto the bed. Turning his back on the clothing, he strode into the bathroom and slammed the door.

"I'm behaving like a nervous virgin about to go out on her first date, for God's sake!" he muttered, stepping under the needle-sharp shower spray. Grabbing the bar of soap from the wall dish, he lathered his torso vigorously. "And damned if I'm not talking to myself!"

Some thirty minutes later, showered, shampooed and attired in tan slacks and a brown-and-white shirt, Zack sat musing over a steaming mug of coffee, timing how many waves curled onto the shore in a sixty-second period.

Grunting, he changed position in the rattan chair for the third time. Anticipation leaped like a living thing inside him when the phone shrilled loudly in the too quiet room.

"Hello?" Zack's voice was tinged with cautious hope.

"Morning, Good-lookin'," his sister Kit sang merrily. "Why do I have this feeling you were expecting someone else?"

"Oh, hi, Kit." Zack smiled; he always smiled at the sound of his sister's voice. "And I wasn't expecting to hear from someone else. I was just hoping it was someone else," he admitted dryly.

"You were hoping it was Thackery?"

Zack frowned. He hadn't even been thinking about Thackery. Come to that, he'd barely given a thought to his brother or the letter he'd sent off to him since he'd first noticed Aubrey on the bluff. He admitted as much to his sister.

"Well, actually, I'm not holding much hope of hearing from Thackery anymore. It has been several weeks now, you know."

"Really, Zack," Kit protested. "You don't even know what the man is doing. For all you know, he could be out of the country and possibly hasn't even seen the letter yet."

"You could be right." Zack shrugged, aware that suddenly a meeting with his twin didn't seem quite as important as it once had. "So anyway, how are things proceeding with big, bad Logan?" Zack referred to Kit's father's stepson from a previous marriage. A grin revealed his white teeth when Kit gritted hers.

"Oooh, that man!" Kit exclaimed. "I called him to plead with him to at least come to the casino and meet with Flint Falcon, the man who's interested in buying the place." Kit had to pause to gasp for air. "And would you believe that his foreman actually told me Logan was too busy to come to the phone?"

Zack's grin widened, as a mental image formed of the formidable Logan McKittrick. "Sure," he drawled, revealing his grin in his tone. "I'd believe that."

"It's not funny! I want to get rid of this casino!"

"So sell this Falcon fella your seventy-five percent of the place," Zack advised. "Then take the money and run."

"But that's the problem!" Kit nearly shouted. "Mr. Falcon has decided he wants the whole ball of wax or nothing and, for who knows what reason, Logan is being difficult. Now he claims he's not sure that selling his twenty-five percent interest would be wise." Kit paused to breathe deeply, calmingly. "Honestly, Zack, I could just slug Logan!"

"I wouldn't advise it, babe." Zack laughed softly. "He just might slug you back."

"And then *you'd* have to come to Nevada to defend me," Kit gibed.

"Who me?" Zack managed a note of shock around his amusement. "You have got to be kidding. Godzilla would hesitate before taking on Logan McKittrick!" Zack was only half joking. He liked and admired the rugged rancher and, though he didn't really fear Logan, he had a healthy respect for the big man.

"Some protective older brother you turned out to be," Kit moaned. "What am I going to do about Logan?"

"Wrap him around your little finger," Zack said. "As you've always done to the both of us. Logan's always been as much of a sucker for your sweet act as I have been." He laughed again. "And he should know better. Hell, Logan's three years older than me."

"Logan's already informed me that this time the sweet talk won't work," Kit mumbled. "Darn his black Scottish hide!"

Zack laughed outright. "So Logan's finally got your number, has he? Well, hang in there, baby sister. You'll think of some way to bring him around." His laughter thinned to an indulgent chuckle. "You usually do."

"Fat lot of help you are," Kit complained. "Zack, you can't imagine how much I dislike running this casino. I sometimes wish Dad had left the whole blasted thing to Logan."

"No, you don't," Zack contradicted.

"No, I don't." Kit sighed. "In any case, how are things going with you, big brother?"

An image of Aubrey, her eyes haunted and wary, flashed into his mind. "At the moment, slow to stop." Zack's lips curved wryly.

"You're not working?"

Working? Zack smiled. *Only on an extremely skittish woman.* He kept the observation to himself. "I, ah, have a few projects in mind." He thought it prudent not to mention that those projects concerned a sad-eyed woman and a bed. "But so far they're only in my head."

"You'll get results, Zack," Kit said earnestly. "You always do."

God, he hoped so! "I'm encouraged by your faith in me," he replied dryly.

They spoke for several more minutes, Zack teasing, as usual, Kit retaliating, also as usual.

Zack glanced at his wristwatch as he replaced the receiver. Seven-twenty. Still too early to go knocking on motel room doors. Taut with impatience, he shot out of the chair and into the roomy, well-equipped kitchen. After refilling his coffee mug, he slid a stool out from under the breakfast bar that separated the kitchen from the small, intimate dining area. Dropping onto the stool, he propped his elbows on the smooth wood surface of the bar and cradled the mug in his broad hands.

How much longer should he wait? Zack wondered. How much longer *could* he wait? He wanted to see her, talk to her, simply *be* with her.

The yearning to share time with another person was unusual; the longing to be with a particular woman—if only to talk—was startling.

Zack had known, in all definitions of the word, many women. In fact, he had broken contact with the last of those women less than a month before. A wry smile twitched his lips as he thought of the platinum blonde he'd secretly dubbed "The Compleat Socialite." Not at any given time had he felt this impatient longing to be with the Palm Springs heiress, not even when they were alone in his bedroom, au naturel.

The consideration spurred speculative thoughts of Aubrey in similar circumstances, her glorious black mane fanned out on his pillow.

Zack drank deeply from his mug, scalding his tongue in the process.

"Damn!" Muttering harshly, he squirmed on the padded stool.

Another quick glance at his watch informed him that all of ten minutes had passed. Blowing on the steaming brew, Zack issued a mental order to think of something—anything—else.

But what? The silent reply came as he slid off the stool and ambled over to the glass wall in the living room. He *could* give some serious consideration to the partially completed statue of the knight errant lying abandoned on his work bench on the floor above.

Zack thought about finishing the piece for all of eighteen seconds before the vision of the small statue was replaced by the body and soul-stirring image of a sad-eyed, black-haired trespasser.

Again he glanced at his watch, groaning as he realized that only four and a half minutes had passed. Beginning to feel desperate, he searched for diversion. The sight of the phone brought back his conversation with Kit, and her mention of his twin brother, Thackery.

Thackery. What was he like? Zack mused, trying to envision another man with his own features. Did Thackery stand the same six feet four inches in height that he himself did? Was his skin the same burnished bronze color? Did he have the exact shade of white-gold hair? Was his frame as muscularly slim as Zack's own? Was Thackery's face clean shaven or did he sport the same type of narrow, closely trimmed beard as Zack did?

Gazing at the waves being tossed against the rocky bluff, Zack smiled as he remembered the countless times he'd wondered about the twin he hadn't seen in thirty years. Understandably, there were and continued to be times when Zack longed for the sight of the brother his mother had said was his mirror image.

Was there a woman in his brother's life? Zack's smile widened. There was if Thackery was anything like Zack emotionally. For in all truth, Zack honestly liked women. He even believed in the possibility of a lasting relationship between a man and a woman—as long as it was the right man and woman.

Woman. *Aubrey*. Zack sighed. In the limited amount of time he'd spent with her, Aubrey had impressed Zack as decidedly "all woman." But there was something or someone haunting her, shadowing her violet eyes, robbing the color from her satiny cheeks.

A man? Zack's eyebrows drew together and his lips turned down. Had some insensitive man hurt Aubrey? Perhaps used her, then cast her aside?

The sudden burst of fury that roared through Zack's mind and body at the mere thought of another man touching Aubrey, let alone mishandling her, was so very intense that he was forced to push his hands into his pants pockets to keep from slamming his fist into the wall.

Shocked by his reaction, Zack stood very still, breathing slowly, deliberately. Then, the need to see her uppermost in his mind, he strode to the door to the outside stairway.

Zack didn't understand the magnetic pull that drew him to seek Aubrey out; he didn't understand the strength of the attraction that had drawn him to her the moment he'd first seen her on the stage of that small San Francisco club. Hell, for all he knew, Aubrey could possess the intelligence of a flea!

Zack shook his head as he took the steps two at a time.

He didn't need to understand. He didn't need to know. Understanding would come with time; knowledge would come with understanding. Right now, all he needed was to see Aubrey.

The light rap against the door startled Aubrey out of the restless slumber she'd drifted into less than four hours earlier. Confused, she peered around the room through eyelids tight and swollen from weeping. A second, sharper rap against the wood drew her bleary gaze to the door.

Who the devil... Even as the thought formed, Zack called to her softly.

"Aubrey?"

"Just...just a minute, please." Dragging her emotion-depleted body from the bed, Aubrey stared down at herself in blank amazement; she had slept in her clothes! As she padded barefoot to the door, she raked her fingers through her disheveled hair, wincing when her nails caught in the tangled waves.

Her hands were unsteady as she fumbled with the night lock and safety chain. The tightly drawn drapes had kept the room in semidarkness; Aubrey blinked against the glare of morning sunlight when she pulled the door open.

"Good morning."

Aubrey blinked again at the sound of Zack's low, yet fully alert, voice. Bathed in sunlight, he seemed to glow with fresh-scrubbed cleanliness and robust good health. Aubrey immediately felt unkempt and decidedly sickly.

"What time is it?" The precise tone she strove for came out in a mumble.

Zack arched his brows over eyes bright with amazement. "Time for breakfast," he said teasingly. "May I come in?" He performed an amazing trick of lowering one brow while arching the other higher still.

Aubrey stared at his brows in mute fascination for a moment, then shook her head. "No!" Now her tone aimed at firmness and came out in a nervous squeak. "I, ah, I'm not ready! I mean, I must shower, and, and..." She grimaced as she looked down at her rumpled clothes. "I fell asleep in my clothes." As she explained, she asked herself why she was bothering. This man meant nothing to her. She didn't owe him an explanation—did she? Nevertheless, she blundered on. "I must change."

Throughout her disjointed chatter Zack contented himself with smiling at her from brown eyes alive with interest. Aubrey was forced to stifle the urge to slam the door in his handsome face. Still, she had agreed to join him for breakfast and a guided tour of the gallery. Sighing, she let her head drop forward to rest on the solid wood panel. Instantly the sparkle disappeared from Zack's laughing brown eyes and was replaced by dark shadows of concern.

"Are you all right?"

A smile appeared on her colorless lips. "Yes, Zack, I'm all right. A little tired, but all right." Squaring her shoulders, she straightened away from the door. "If you'll give me half an hour, I'll meet you in the restaurant."

Zack frowned. "I think I'd rather hang around out here."

"But—" Aubrey began.

"You're wasting time," he interrupted, "And I'm hungry." A smile softened his mouth. "Will you get it together?"

Aubrey smiled back despite her weariness. "Okay. I'll be as quick as possible."

Exactly twenty-eight minutes were required to shower, dress, lightly make up her face and untangle her hair with the concentrated effort of a ruthlessly applied brush. As she ran a final critical glance over her reflection in the bathroom mirror, Aubrey decided she looked as though she just might live.

After checking to make sure her room key was in her purse, she pulled the door shut, her gaze sweeping the area for a tall, golden man. Zack was standing at the edge of the road, his tall frame hunched over as he bent to converse with the occupant of a car. As Aubrey approached him he laughed and rose to his full height. A hand waved from the car window as the vehicle drove away.

"Friends of yours?" she asked as she came to a halt beside him.

"No, tourists." Zack angled his head to gaze down at her. "They wanted to know how much farther it was to Monterey." His eyes warmed as he surveyed her appearance in close-fitting white jeans and a loosely knit pullover in shocking pink. As his gaze returned to her eyes he did the eyebrow trick again. "How did you do that?"

"Do what?" Aubrey asked blankly.

"That complete change." His hand moved languidly to indicate her small form. "A half hour ago you looked like the morning after the night before." Zack favored her with his heaven-sent smile. "And now you look like a confection whipped up by a French chef."

"Why, thank you!" Flustered, Aubrey lowered her black lashes, then, slowly, she swept her glance up the length of his body. The light breeze molded the tan slacks to his legs, revealing well-developed calves and tightly muscled thighs. A narrow leather belt enhanced his small waist and slender hips. Her lashes fluttered as her gaze moved up over his flatly muscled chest and broad shoulders and the triangle of gold skin and hair exposed at the open neck of his shirt.

Her breath caught as her glance moved over his handsome face. "You, ah..." Her gaze followed the gold line of the closely trimmed, narrow beard that delineated his strong jawline. She had never been kissed by a man with a beard. The thought brought a flush of color to Aubrey's normally pale cheeks.

"Yes?" There was a waiting, breathless note to Zack's tone.

Aubrey's gaze lifted to meet his eyes, and froze in the hot brown depths. Speaking was a major accomplishment.

"Y-you hardly have the look of an undercooked hamburger from a fast food drivethrough," she whispered, inwardly groaning at the idiocy of the remark.

Zack's quiet laughter did amazing and wonderful things to her spine. "Not exactly chopped liver?" he teased.

"A far cry from that." His laughter sparked a smile from her. "And you know it," she added, matching his teasing tone.

Zack's shrug was easy and relaxed and yet classically elegant. "My mother was very beautiful," he explained, looping one arm over her shoulders as he started across the road. "And if you think I'm pretty, you should see my sister." The glance he slanted down at her was alive with deviltry.

Responding to his sense of fun, Aubrey felt the tension of the previous day ease out of her. She walked beside him quietly until they reached the middle of the road, then her gaze drifted in the direction of the car Zack had been bending over when she left her room.

"Is it very far to Monterey?" Interest was woven through her tone.

"No." Zack was quiet until they stepped onto the parking area of his own property before continuing. "You've never been to Monterey?"

Aubrey shook her head. "No. As a matter of fact, this is my first visit to the West Coast."

Zack came to a stop at the base of the stone stairs that led to the first level of the complex. "Your first visit from where?"

"The East Coast," she replied simply.

"Specifically?" His right eyebrow inched into an arch.

Aubrey couldn't contain the burst of soft laughter that rippled from her throat. "Philadelphia," she sputtered. "And how do you manage that eyebrow thing?"

"I taught myself to do it by practicing in front of a mirror when I was a kid." Zack grinned, releasing his hold on her by trailing his finger over her shoulders and down her arm. As his palm slid over hers, he laced their fingers together. Then, tugging gently on her hand, he started up the steps.

"Did you?" Aubrey asked skeptically. "Really?"

"Sure." Zack's grin widened. "I saw an actor do it in a movie and thought it was neat. I practiced for weeks before I had it down pat. Now it comes naturally."

Aubrey slid a bemused glance over his face as she mounted the steps beside him. Though his features were smooth and relaxed, his lips were tilted in wry amusement. On consideration, Aubrey couldn't think of any man she knew with the panache to admit to a polished affectation.

The warmth from his hand spread to encompass her entire body. She was beginning to really like this man, she realized in surprise.

Zackery Sharp was a genuinely nice man, she decided as they crossed the courtyard to the restaurant.

The first thing Aubrey noticed when they entered the restaurant was the absence of customers. The place was completely deserted. As Zack guided her to a table by the windows, she frowned in confusion. Zack raised one eyebrow questioningly.

"Where is everybody?"

"Everybody?" he repeated. "Who were you expecting?"

Distracted, Aubrey missed the note of amusement in his tone. "People," she responded vaguely, glancing around the empty room. "Customers. Patrons having breakfast."

"The restaurant never serves breakfast."

"Never serves breakfast!" Aubrey blinked. "But—"

"The restaurant opens for lunch at eleven o'clock," Zack interrupted.

"But then what are we doing here?" Aubrey asked blankly.

"I have breakfast here most mornings." Zack flashed his disarming smile. "I own the place, you know." He shrugged. "The staff arrives around eight to begin preparing the lunch menu. I usually wander in about eight-thirty.''

Aubrey relaxed against the curved-back chair. Being alone in the large room felt odd, but not uncomfortable. A teasing smile played over her soft lips. ''Does having the place to yourself every morning make you feel sorta like the king of the hill?''

Zack's soft laughter added warmth to the attractive room. ''Sorta.'' He surprised her with the admission, making her wonder again how many men would own up to the feeling. ''I won't deny that I rather enjoy the fuss made over me here.''

''You're not exactly humble,'' Aubrey taunted gently, ''are you, Mr. Sharp?''

''I'm not at all humble, Miss Mason,'' Zack replied, arching one brow. ''Or is it Mrs. Mason?'' Though his tone was smooth, the question he asked was pointed.

Aubrey felt the effect of his probing stare in every nerve ending in her body. She wet her suddenly dry lips with the tip of her tongue. Heat coursed through her body as his narrow-eyed gaze followed her unconsciously sensual action.

"Sorry to keep you waiting, Mr. Sharp."

A sigh of relief whispered past Aubrey's lips at the timely arrival of the waitress.

"No apology necessary, Ruth," Zack murmured. "We're not in a hurry."

As the waitress handed them menus, Aubrey echoed Zack's reassurance to the woman with a warm smile. Ruth smiled back easily.

"Would you like coffee while you decide?"

"Yes, please."

"And juice," Zack added.

The instant the waitress moved away, Zack returned his drilling stare to Aubrey. "You didn't answer my question," he said tersely. "Is it Miss or Mrs.?"

"Either one would be correct, I suppose," Aubrey replied. "I'm a widow, Zack."

So there had been a man. The confirmation of his earlier speculation caused a twisting sensation in the pit of Zack's stomach. The image of her kneeling on the bluff sprang into his mind. And that haunted look that came into her eyes . . . Was she grieving, or . . . ?

Ignoring the physical and mental discomfort, Zack leaned against the back of his chair lazily. "I'm sorry." He sighed silently at the note of insincerity on his tone. Speculation stirred anew at the humorless smile that briefly touched her lips.

"Thank you, but..." Aubrey turned away to glance out the window; Zack was positive she didn't see the magnificence of the view.

"But?" he probed when she failed to continue.

"It's been three years now." Aubrey sighed as she swung her gaze back to him. "The marriage was over long before the accident."

Zack couldn't deny the shiver of relief that moved from the back of his neck to the base of his spine. Her quietly controlled voice echoed in his mind. *It was over long before the...*

"Accident?" he asked alertly, sitting up straight.

"Yes, a boating accident." Aubrey feigned interest in the menu, cringing inside with the searing memory. Even as she prayed that he would let the subject drop, she knew he wouldn't. She was right.

"How did the accident happen?"

Her appetite gone, Aubrey pushed the menu aside. "A sudden freak storm," she said tightly. Lowering her gaze to avoid the concern flaring in Zack's eyes, she toyed with the slender stem on the small juice glass.

"You weren't with him?" Zack inquired tersely.

Aubrey shook her head. "No, I was working. I didn't even know he—Keith—had taken the boat out." Lifting the glass, she gulped a large swallow of the juice to relieve the sudden dryness in her throat. "I—I wasn't even aware of the approaching storm." She betrayed the tension tautening her nerves by the careful way she set the glass on the table.

"Aubrey—" Zack began softly.

"Ready to order?" The waitress's cheerful voice interrupted.

Aubrey flinched, but covered it quickly with a smile. "I don't think—"

"Yes, Ruth," Zack inserted smoothly. "Bring two ham and cheese omelets, please."

"Toast? Croissants? Muffins?" Ruth asked as she refilled their cups from the ceramic carafe she was holding.

"Yes." Zack grinned. "Bring some of each."

"You shouldn't have done that," Aubrey protested after Ruth moved away from the table.

Zack managed a careless shrug. "Why not? I like all three."

"I wasn't referring to the bread and pastries, and you know it." Aubrey raised reproachful eyes to his.

"Yes, I know," Zack agreed easily, then countered, "but I'm concerned about you."

Aubrey frowned. "Concerned?" she repeated. "Why? In what way?"

Zack brought his hand up from the table in a sweeping gesture that encompassed her slight frame. "You have a hollow, fragile look," he explained. "When was the last time you ate anything solid?"

"Ah..." Aubrey's frown deepened with concentration. "I'm not sure, but I think it was at breakfast yesterday."

It was a blatant lie; Aubrey knew full well she had not consumed a thing but coffee the previous day. She also knew that had she tried to eat she'd have choked on the food. Still, it really wasn't any of Zack's business—was it? she reminded herself with rising irritation.

Zack was obviously unimpressed with the defiance blazing from her eyes.

"Are you deliberately trying to make yourself ill?" he asked in a deceptively mild tone.

Aubrey sat up straight, her eyes wide with surprise. "Of course not!" she denied hotly.

"Then—" Zack began, only to pause when Ruth swept up to the table, a large tray in her hands.

Zack bantered with Ruth while she arranged the food, then pinned Aubrey with a narrow-eyed stare the instant they were alone again.

"Then why aren't you eating?"

"I haven't stopped eating!" Aubrey insisted, flushing as the delicious aroma of the food caused her stomach to growl. "It was only yesterday that I couldn't eat," she added wearily, lowering her gaze to her plate.

"Because of your husband?" Zack hated asking the question, and strangely feared hearing her answer. When it came, it pleased and confused him at the same time.

"No, not because of Keith." Aubrey's voice was little more than a reedy whisper.

"But why then?" Zack blurted, shaking his head in bewilderment.

Picking up her fork, Aubrey stabbed at the egg mixture on her plate. Staring at her action as if fascinated by the process of mangling an omelet, she fought an inner battle before glancing up at him.

"Though our marriage was over, I certainly didn't wish Keith any harm," she finally explained. "But I..." She paused to swallow. "I can't pretend to a grief I no longer feel."

The relief that washed through Zack was staggering. It didn't show. Calmly, coolly, as if it hardly mattered, he probed more deeply.

"Then why the fast?" Zack's body grew chilled by the spasm of agony that twisted her face. Without conscious volition, his hand moved to grasp hers. "Aubrey?"

She shook her head in a distracted manner. "I'm all right." Her smile was self-deprecating, and heart wrenching. "Zack, I didn't only lose Keith that day. I—I lost my daughter, too."

Four

Oh, hell. Zack's fingers tightened convulsively on hers. What did a man say in response to a statement like the one Aubrey had made? he asked himself bleakly. "I'm sorry" seemed too trite. "How dreadful" seemed too profuse. "You poor dear" seemed too patronizing.

"Aubrey, I—"

"Your breakfast is getting cold." Aubrey's overly bright tone cut across the deep concern in Zack's lowered voice. With a show that he was positive was pure bravado, she determinedly sliced the edge of her fork through the omelet. Her eyes met his as she brought the small piece to her mouth. "Zack, please, eat your meal."

What could he do? Not a damned thing, he decided, following her example. As he methodically consumed the food, barely tasting it, Zack kept asking himself the same question: What does losing a child do to a parent?

Unbidden, a picture of his mother formed in his mind. The lovely Laureen had always laughed as if she hadn't a care in the world.

Zack glanced at Aubrey's face. Instinct assured him that Aubrey didn't laugh often.

But then of course Laureen hadn't actually *lost* a child—she had thrown him away.

"You're sitting there feeling sorry for me, and I don't like it."

Zack's thoughts were pulled sharply by the intensity of Aubrey's soft voice. His skin felt suddenly warm and prickly, and with a sense of shock, he realized he was flushing guiltily.

Amazing! He hadn't flushed, guiltily or any other way, since passing his thirteenth birthday!

"I'm sorry," he murmured, "but you're only partially right." Zack smiled ruefully. "I was feeling sorry for you, yes, but I was also wondering about my mother, and the way she reacted to similar circumstances.''

''Your mother lost one of her children?''

Zack was shaking his head negatively before Aubrey finished speaking. ''Not lost,'' he corrected cynically. ''My mother gave one of her children away.''

''*Gave* one away?'' Aubrey repeated, her eyes wide with disbelief. ''I don't understand.''

A soft sigh of exasperation whispered through Zack's lips. Dammit, why hadn't he kept his mouth shut? Now he was forced to explain the whole stupid mess. Might as well get it over with.

''Well, you see, I'm the youngest, by eight minutes, of twin boys....''

Her attention was focused entirely on Zack as he related the story of his mother and her decision to separate her five-year-old-twin sons when she left West Texas. With her dizzy logic, Laureen figured that the fair thing to do was leave one twin and take the other twin with her. Aubrey absently finished her meal and nodded her thanks when Ruth refilled their empty coffee cups.

"So I was brought to California with mother, and Thackery was left behind in Texas with our father," Zack concluded.

"And you've never seen or contacted him since?" Aubrey asked in a tone of sheer astonishment.

"That's correct—at least it was until recently." Zack paused to sip at the fresh, hot liquid, then, unconsciously, he sighed again. "The terms of mother's will necessitated contacting Thackery. Along with the legal letter that was sent to him, I included a personal note." He smiled wryly. "Thackery has not responded to either letter."

"But, Zack, surely you won't give up!" Aubrey exclaimed in shock. "Call him or write to him again," she insisted heatedly, unaware that his story had drawn her completely out of her own depressing memories. "You simply can't let it drop, not now."

"Umm," Zack murmured noncommittally. Watching her, he felt a curl of satisfaction unwind inside. Aubrey's face was alive with animation and interest and glowingly beautiful.

"What does 'umm' mean?"

Zack laughed at the indignant sound of Aubrey's voice. "It means I'll consider your advice," he said solemnly.

"But—"

"But first," he interrupted her teasingly, "I'm going to give you the promised tour of my gallery." Pushing his chair back, Zack extended his hand to her as he stood up. "That is, if you still want it." A grin tugging at his lips, he arched one brow tauntingly.

Aubrey wanted to argue, but she also longed for the tour he'd promised her. Smiling at him, she rose and slipped her hand into his.

"We will continue this discussion later," she warned him as she walked out of the restaurant into the bright fall sunlight.

"I was afraid you'd say that," Zack drawled, adjusting his long stride to her much shorter one.

Zack led Aubrey down to the gallery, which was located on the ground level of the four-story complex. Forming the base of the structure, it jutted out beyond the upper stories and the exposed roof was made almost exclusively of glass.

Upon entering the gallery, Aubrey realized that the setup was quite unlike that of any art gallery she'd ever visited. The space was partitioned into four rooms, three of which were lit by the diffused sunlight pouring in through the treated glass panels overhead.

Aubrey was fascinated at once by the beauty of the work displayed. Her sharp, indrawn breath of delight brought a smile of satisfaction to Zack's lips.

"You approve of the layout?"

Aubrey sent her dazzled gaze skipping over the treasures on pedestals. "It's fantastic," she complimented him in a tone of hushed awe. "My father would think he'd died and gone to cultural heaven."

Zack's burst of laughter reverberated through the silent interior of the empty rooms. "Your father is welcome here anytime."

Aubrey tilted her head to give him a sparkling look. "For a guided tour by the great man himself?" she asked teasingly.

Ensnared by the animation lighting her face, Zack could only manage a nod of assent as he stared at her in wonder. Lit from within with humor, Aubrey's violet eyes blazed jewellike in her pale face. A tangled mass of emotions and sensations rushed through his body to create a sensation of warmth in his chest.

So, Zack thought distractedly, *this is what falling in love feels like.*

In love? Zack was narrowing his eyes as he considered the errant idea when Aubrey's chiding voice shattered the stillness inside him.

"Well, are we just going to stand here?" Her gaze again swept the area. "I want to see everything."

I want to kiss you. Zack caught the words before they could pass his lips. Cautioning himself against haste, he reclaimed the small hand he'd released to unlock the door to the gallery.

"And you will," he assured her quietly, "for a price."

"A price?" Aubrey frowned up at him. There was a tiny flame in the depths of his dark eyes that momentarily robbed her of breath. "Wh-what is the cost?" she finally managed in a half gasp.

"Dinner. With me. Tonight. In Monterey." Zack laced their fingers as he succinctly issued his terms, then held his breath as he waited for her response. Fortunately he didn't have to wait long.

"Monterey!" Aubrey laughed. "I'll happily pay the price." She tugged lightly on his hand. "Begin, Mr. Sharp."

Oh, but I have begun, Ms. Mason, Zack thought, moving toward the nearest pedestal. "This piece is the work of an as-yet unknown." Zack indicated the small bronze likeness of an Arabian horse.

"Beautiful." As she breathed the one word of appreciation, Aubrey stepped closer to the statue. "The detail is exquisite." She raised her free hand, then hesitated. "May I touch?"

"Anything that takes your fancy," Zack murmured dryly.

Something in his tone drew her from her absorption with the finely executed sculpture. The force of his dark-eyed gaze rocked her to her foundations. But before she could decide if he meant what she thought he meant, Zack continued calmly.

"As you'll no doubt notice, this particular piece was fashioned by very talented hands." As he spoke, Zack stroked the bronze with his long fingers.

A shiver tingled from Aubrey's nape to the base of her spine. Her gaze riveted on his stroking fingers, she could actually feel his touch on her skin. Incredulity widened her eyes at the depth of yearning that swamped her senses. Unbelievable as it seemed, Aubrey was suddenly aching to experience the caress of Zack's work-roughened hands. Feeling helpless and confused, she mutely observed the action of his fingers.

"The artist is a young woman."

The uncanny spell was broken by Zack's softly spoken words. Snapped back to reality, Aubrey blinked before returning her gaze to his smiling face.

"She is very talented." Even as she stated the obvious, Aubrey felt herself being lost within the warmth of Zack's fire-sparked brown eyes.

"Yes, she is." Though his voice held firm, Zack felt himself drowning in a shimmering sea of violet. Hanging on to coherency, he went on doggedly. "She's a local resident. In my opinion, her name will rank with the finest sculptors someday."

"I'll pass the information along to my father," Aubrey said, vaguely irritated. "What is her name?"

"Riana Dawn." Zack's expression was somber for an instant, then a grin flashed to bring a teasing light to his eyes. "Believe it or not, it *is* her given name."

The sensuously coiled tension eased out of Aubrey, leaving in its wake the conflicting sensations of emptiness and relief. Attempting to ignore the former, she latched on to the latter with a forced laugh. "Given or assumed, it's a beautiful name."

"Yes," Zack agreed softly. "Almost as beautiful as Aubrey."

The slender fingers captured inside his broad hand trembled. Zack gently tightened his grasp. Things were moving too quickly. He was making her wary of him. He knew he should ease up, yet everything male inside him urged a more intimate contact with her. Aubrey decided the issue for him by slipping her hand from his and walking away.

"And what have we here?" Deploring the thready sound of her voice, Aubrey cleared her throat as she came to a halt at the next pedestal. The carved wood piece on display was modernistic and smoothly arresting.

Zack was laughing easily as he came to a stop beside her. "Here we have the finished product of a very avant-garde mind." His laughter ceased as he contemplated the oddly shaped object. "I have a distinct feeling that this man—" he indicated the piece as if implying the artist and the work were one and the same "—will electrify the art world before too long."

As had happened previously, Aubrey stared at him in wonder. Not the slightest hint of envy tinged Zack's tone. His relaxed expression signaled an inner satisfaction. Didn't Zack feel at all threatened? Aubrey mused, searching his face for a shadow of professional envy. The shadow simply did not exist. On reflection, Aubrey was convinced that Zack was free of any covetous emotion. He was secure in and with his own talent. Yes, she mentally reiterated her earlier opinion—Zackery Sharp was a really *nice* person.

"You stand stunned before greatness?"

Zack's nudging query brought a smile to Aubrey's lips and a sparkle to her eyes. Slanting a glance at him, she unconsciously admitted more than she wished to. "I do stand stunned before you."

Zack went as still as any of the pieces of artistic endeavor on display. Wondering precisely what she meant, and almost afraid to ask, he studied her for long seconds. "You consider me touched by greatness?'' His emotion-roughened voice was little more than a murmur.

"How could you doubt it when every art critic in the world proclaims you great?'' Aubrey tried for a light, chiding tone. "And answer honestly, Zack. Don't go all humble on me now.'' The quaver in her voice convinced her she'd been less than successful with her attempt at humor.

"Me? Humble?'' Zack gave a short bark of laughter. "I wouldn't know where to begin.'' His laughter subsiding, he leveled a piercing stare at her. "Besides which, I don't give a damn what the critics think. What I'm curious about is *your* opinion.''

The tension was back in double force and it sent sensations skimming along her nerves, dancing down her spine. The realization that Zack was dead serious heightened the tension, and the awareness of how close he was standing to her rocketed through her body. Having charged him with being honest, Aubrey knew she had to be truthful in her reply to him.

"Yes, Zack,'' she answered clearly. "I'm positive that you've been touched by greatness.''

An odd, quivering sensation rippled over Zack's shoulders and down his arms. Contrary to his adamant denial, he felt inordinately humbled by her assertion . . . exactly as he had by her praise of his work in the courtyard the afternoon before. Inclining his head, Zack ran an assessing glance over her small, slim form. A strange tightness gripped his throat. The sight of her pleased him in an almost painful way.

"Thank you." Zack was aware of the inadequacy of his response, yet it was all he could force through the emotion tightening his throat.

"You're welcome." Like a bow being tautened by increments, the tension increased in Aubrey. Zack's softened expression was playing havoc with her equilibrium. Without conscious direction, her hand sought his. Aubrey felt the earth right itself when his hand grasped hers.

"Aubrey."

Her name. A whisper. A lure that tangled her emotions and ensnared her undivided attention. Aubrey found the simple act of swallowing extremely difficult.

"Yes?"

Zack's lips quirked in self-derision. "Nothing, just *Aubrey*."

"Nothing, just Aubrey," had the power to weaken her knees. The arrival of the curator Zack employed saved her the ignominy of sinking to the floor at his feet.

The remainder of the guided tour was highly anticlimactic. Zack's voice was brisk as he returned the curator's greeting. After a hasty introduction to the man, Zack swept Aubrey away to view the gleaming works of art. Fortunately, the curator, a middle-aged gentleman named Carl Jensen, didn't appear either surprised or affronted by his employer's precipitous action.

"You were rude, Zack." Aubrey addressed the chastising comment to a matt-finished pentagon-shaped piece of dark wood, which stood at an angle, surrounded by narrow strips of curled metal.

"I know." Zack sighed. "I was annoyed by the interruption."

Aubrey kept her gaze fastened to the seemingly freestanding sculpture. "And are you always rude when you're annoyed?"

"Most times," he admitted shamelessly. "But in my own defense, I must add that I'm not easily annoyed."

Detecting his smile from his tone, Aubrey felt her lips twitch in response. "I will remember to try not to annoy you," she said lightly, frowning at the pentagon.

"Good." Zack's murmur came from directly behind her; Aubrey concentrated on the sculpture. "This piece fascinates you?" One arm shot by her face as he reached around her to stroke the dull wood.

Tactile. The word sprang into Aubrey's mind as she experienced again the yearning to feel the touch of his fingers. But of course, she reasoned, as a sculptor Zack would appreciate all forms of textures... wood, metal, stone, skin—Aubrey felt a shiver feather hers.

"I—" She forced her mind to consider his question. "This piece baffles me," she admitted candidly.

Zack laughed. "You're not the first to confess confusion about it."

An underlying note in his tone tipped her off to his own ambiguity regarding the work. "You don't like it, either, do you?"

"No, I don't," Zack said bluntly. "But then I don't have to like it. I merely have to recognize the talent behind it."

Nice. Tactile. Aubrey added the word *complex* to her growing list of descriptive adjectives applying to Zack. Prudently, she avoided the word *sexy*—had she not, it would have topped the list.

Zack watched and listened as Aubrey and he walked from the pedestals to long tables that held groupings of large and small sculptures. Casually, innocuously, he drew her out by urging her to state her opinion. Aubrey's knowledge of art amazed him, her decisiveness as to her likes and dislikes delighted him.

It was past noon when Zack ushered Aubrey from the controlled light of the gallery into the glare of afternoon sunshine.

"I'm starving." Zack made the announcement as the door closed behind them with a muted click.

Aubrey blinked against the bright light. Surprised, she realized that she was also quite hungry. "You know, I'm hungry, too!" she exclaimed.

Though he remained silent, Zack slanted a shrewd glance at her as he led the way up the steps to the restaurant level. The glow on Aubrey's face ignited a corresponding glow deep inside his body. The warmth comprised elements both sensual and sentimental. Aubrey was hungry, and he had helped bring about the phenomenon. Satisfaction rushed through his veins with heated urgency. If he could arouse one type of hunger, Zack mused, there was the possibility he was capable of arousing another, more earthy, hunger in her. The prospect was almost shocking in its excitement value. Tamping down a searing flare of need, Zack held the restaurant door for her to precede him into the room.

Lunch was delicious. Seasoned by a lively discussion of the works they'd spent the morning examining, the spinach salads they ordered disappeared swiftly, as did the bottle of California Chardonnay Zack had insisted they have to accompany the meal.

The meal finished, Zack and Aubrey strolled around the courtyard, coming to a stop at the large copper statue as if by mutual agreement.

Eyes narrowed in concentration, Aubrey slowly circled the statue in silence. Wryly amused, while at the same time oddly anxious, Zack waited patiently for her to complete her circle. As she rejoined him, Aubrey stared up at him contemplatively. When she finally spoke, her tone was threaded with solid belief.

"You know, the objects we looked at this morning are brilliantly crafted," she said slowly. "But by comparison, your work makes them pale."

Considering the source, for Zack this was the ultimate praise. Speechless for perhaps the first time in his adult life, Zack merely stared into Aubrey's somber eyes, listening to a chant grow demandingly louder inside his head: *I want this woman in my life.* In a bid to silence the chant, Zack responded flippantly.

"It's the shiny copper."

Aubrey burst out laughing. "Zackery Sharp!" she gasped. "Do you ever take anything seriously?"

"Not if I can avoid it." Laughing with her, he grasped her hand and started down the stairs to the road.

"Where are we going now?" Aubrey asked curiously, following without resistance.

"Back to the motel," Zack replied without pausing. "I'd like to leave for Monterey in exactly—" he turned his wrist to glance at the slim gold watch encircling it "—one hour." He arched one eyebrow as he glanced over his shoulder. "Is that okay with you?" A coaxing grin flashed briefly.

Endearing. Aubrey added another adjective to her list.

"Yes, Zack, that will be okay with me." Aubrey grinned back at him, then yelped as she crashed into his hard body when he came to an abrupt halt. "Zackery, what...?" Her voice faded on a sputter.

"You know," Zack murmured contemplatively, "I have known some exceptionally beautiful women." Leaning back, he slowly surveyed her form with a warm gaze. "But by comparison, you make them all pale."

Aubrey's heartbeat and breathing came to full stop, then accelerated to an alarming rate. Flushed with pleasure, she stared at him. The tiny flame in his dark eyes flared into a raging blaze. Afraid he might kiss her, afraid that he wouldn't, she slowly lowered her eyelids. She felt cold when he stepped back, away from her.

"Come along." Zack gave a gentle tug on her hand. "The hour has now been cut to fifty-five minutes."

Quivering inside and outside, Aubrey docilely trailed him down the footpath and stairs. By exerting sheer willpower, she had her rattled emotions under control when they reached the door to her motel room. Her composure intact, Aubrey smiled and nodded when Zack advised her to hurry.

"I'll be back in fifty minutes," he warned, turning to lope across the motel parking lot.

"I'll be ready," Aubrey promised serenely, before dashing into the room, slamming the door and making a frantic beeline for the connecting bathroom.

Not once did Aubrey pause to question her unusual response to the sun-burnished, confusing giant who had seemingly effortlessly swept her out of her self-absorption. There was simply no time for introspection.

White jeans and pink top went sailing through the air as Aubrey literally tore the clothes from her body. She didn't have time to question; Zack would be coming for her in forty-odd minutes.

Love. Was it possible? Zack backed into the pulsating shower spray. Jets of hot water beat against his nape while the recurring question beat inside his head. Was it possible that he was falling in love with a woman he barely knew?

At the thought of Aubrey, her face animated, her violet eyes alive with interest, a fine layer of goose bumps erupted on his skin, defying the warmth of the water cascading over his body.

Zack had always believed in the theory of deep, abiding love between one man and one woman. He'd even had brief moments when he'd almost thought he'd found it. Searing disappointment had accompanied the discovery that he had been wrong.

A small smile of satisfaction curved his lips as he twisted the water taps off and stepped from the shower stall. Now, having met Aubrey, he was grateful he'd realized he'd been mistaken about the depth of the affection he'd felt for previous women. Now, having met Aubrey, Zack understood the difference, infinite in scope, between affection and the more exciting, complex emotion known as love.

Yes, it was possible to fall in love so quickly. Zack grinned at his reflected image in the steam-clouded mirror. Before him shimmered the naked proof of that possibility.

Whistling softly through his teeth, Zack tossed the sodden bath towel into the white wicker hamper in the corner and strolled into the bedroom.

Loving Aubrey would not be easy, he mused, absently choosing a pale blue shirt to match the navy slacks he drew up over his slim hips. Or, more accurately, convincing Aubrey to love and be loved would not be easy. She had a tragic past to resolve, ghosts to be laid to rest. Zack was well aware of the difficulty he faced. But then, who knew better than he how very intrigued he'd always felt when presented with a challenge?

As he stood in front of the dresser mirror to run a brush through his damp hair, Zack narrowed his eyes in contemplation. The urge to sweep Aubrey into the secure haven of his arms was strong. Stronger still was the knowledge that precipitous action on his part would cause her to bolt.

Aubrey was obviously hurting. *Make haste slowly,* Zack advised himself, tossing the brush to the dresser top. During the course of the morning, the haunting shadows in her eyes had been replaced by the sparkle of interest. Might he not recall the shadows if he came on too strong?

Play it with caution, play it cool, he further advised his narrow-eyed image, *or you just might find yourself playing it alone.*

His course set, Zack slid change, car keys and his wallet into his pockets, then loped from the apartment to the garage that made up the fourth and only section of the gallery level that didn't have a glass roof. He was whistling again as he backed the gleaming black Jaguar from its stall.

Five

Aubrey was transferring her "junk" from the soft leather bag to a flat, paisley-patterned purse when she heard the muted roar of the engine and then the solid thunk of a car door being swung shut. Her fingers suddenly unsteady, she scooped up the room key from the low dresser with one hand and grabbed the narrow strap on the purse with the other. Crossing to the door, she pulled it open as Zack was raising one hand to knock.

The sight of him caused the tremor in her fingers to radiate up her arms and to the pit of her stomach. Was it legal for a man to look so good? The whimsical thought flashed through Aubrey's mind as she swept an appreciative glance over his tall frame.

"How refreshing."

Stepping onto the cement walkway beside him, Aubrey frowned as she closed the door behind her. Refreshing? As compliments went, refreshing wasn't the most exciting. Obviously, Zack read her expression like an open book.

"I meant," he said around a half smile, "I find a woman who can be ready on time extremely refreshing." Looping his arm casually around the back of her waist, Zack led her to the car. "And, to discover a *beautiful* woman who can be ready on time is like finding diamonds in a tar pit."

Sly devil! Aubrey thought, averting her face to conceal her twitching lips as she slid onto the supple leather seat. One could certainly not accuse Zackery Sharp of trying to turn her head with blatantly effusive flattery! But, she mused, perhaps his reticence was just as well, considering how very prized she was feeling at that moment.

Watching Zack fit his long frame into the seat behind the wheel, Aubrey felt surprisingly gratified for the care she'd taken in choosing a garment to wear to have dinner with him. The softly feminine, cream-toned skirt with its matching russet-and-tan shawl, complemented the tan jacket he'd donned over the navy slacks and pale blue shirt.

Studying him through lowered lashes, Aubrey's breath caught as the midafternoon sunlight shot sparks of reddish copper off his bronze-gold hair.

"Forget something?" Zack paused in the act of reaching for the ignition key to arch a brow at her.

"No." Aubrey shook her head, in answer and relief, as the sun was obscured by a gray-tinged, fluffy cloud and the copper halo effect was removed.

"Good." A flick of his wrist and the engine growled to life. "Let's go investigate Monterey."

"Yes, let's." Aubrey glanced out the window, then frowned. "I only hope we aren't forced to do our investigating in the rain." Leaning forward, she arced her gaze across the cloud-spattered sky.

"The weather service has predicted a thunderstorm." Zack offered the information as he drove the car off the lot and onto the highway. "But not until later this evening," he went on, after easing the Jaguar around two slower-moving cars. When he'd increased the speed of the car to the legal limit, Zack flashed a teasing grin at her. "It's been known to rain a bit in California this time of year, you know."

"Hmm," Aubrey murmured, tilting her head to give him an amused look. "I've heard about the bit of rainfall California gets in the fall."

Zack laughed. "I'm sure the entire world has heard about our bit of rainfall." Lifting one hand from the wheel, he indicated the surrounding terrain. "But it's not raining now, so enjoy."

A soft "Oh" of delight whispered through Aubrey's parted lips. Up until that point, the road had been shadowed by tree-covered hills rising gently on both sides. As Zack spoke, the car crested a hill. The hills angled off to Aubrey's right, the slope steeper, the vegetation dwindling to low shrubs and bushes. But what drew the gasp of delight from her was the panoramic view to her left, where the hills dropped to form craggy cliffs with a sheer descent to the sea below. Moments later, she drew her breath in sharply as the sun blazed from behind a cloud to dazzle light on the multihued blue Pacific.

"Quite awesome, isn't it?" Zack asked quietly.

"Magnificent," Aubrey breathed, surveying the miles of scenic beauty spread out before them.

"You didn't drive down this way from San Francisco?"

"No." Though she responded absently, Aubrey experienced a twinge as she remembered the drive. On escaping San Francisco, she'd been in search of solitude, not the wonders of nature. "I followed the inland route."

"I'm glad."

"Really?" Aubrey leveled a quizzical look at him. "Why?"

"Because now I have the pleasure of introducing you to all Big Sur has to offer," Zack answered simply. "Have you been to Carmel?"

Fascinated by the play of light in his narrow gold beard, Aubrey shook her head negatively in answer.

"Would you like to stop before going to Monterey?" A smile appeared on his sensuous lips as he caught a glimpse of her rapt expression.

"I—I'd love to stop." Rueing the husky sound of her voice, Aubrey forced her gaze away from his masculine beauty to the less-arousing view of blue ocean and rugged coastline.

As the powerful Jaguar ate up the miles, Zack pointed out and named the most famous landmarks. At one point the cliffs dwindled to uneven terrain.

"Over there—" Zack indicated a humped-back hill that jutted out into the ocean "—is the Point Sur lighthouse."

Aubrey craned her neck to get a glimpse of the building that was set on the downward slope of the hill. Then, as abruptly as they'd dropped away, the craggy cliffs rose majestically again.

"If you look sharp, you might catch sight of the homes nestled into the side of the cliffs," Zack said quietly.

Alerted, Aubrey did manage a flashing peek of a corner of a roof. "The view from that location must be spectacular," she remarked, carefully scanning the cliff sides for evidence of other structures.

"Umm, yes." Zack slanted a smile at her while keeping his steady-eyed gaze on the curving road. "And, as I'm sure you've noticed, the buildings are designed to blend in with the terrain."

"Yes, I had— Oh, my!" Aubrey broke off to exclaim, twisting around in her seat to stare out the back window. "There's one that looks like it's crawling up the side of the cliff!"

Zack laughed softly. "Quite a few of them were constructed that way."

Falling silent, Zack was content to enjoy the pleasure the drive was affording Aubrey. Slicing the occasional quick glance at her glowing face, he renewed his own appreciation of the dazzling coastline by viewing it through her eyes.

The quiet was soothingly companionable for some miles, then Aubrey again shattered it with a softly gasped "Oh, Zack, will you look at that bridge!"

"That's the Bixby Bridge. Impressive, isn't it?"

Straining against the seat belt, Aubrey forgot to reply as she attempted to see both sides of the relatively narrow bridge that was spanned across a wide gorge. The sight of the ground, hundreds of feet below, was dizzying and she was satisfied to settle back in the plush leather seat as the purring car left the span behind.

They were climbing now, as the road curved and clung to the rise of the glissading headlands. Looking ahead and to the left, Aubrey was treated to the sight of the sapphire Pacific spread out before her to where it met the pale blue of the sky at the horizon.

"If we had time, I'd stop at the observation point at Lobos." Zack's quiet tone dissolved her near mesmerized state. "It's an excellent spot for observing tide pool life, sea lions and sea otters, but I want you to see Carmel in the daylight."

Though she was greedy to see all the attractions the coastline had to offer, Aubrey was happy to let Zack set the itinerary. Besides which, she was getting hungry.

"You're the tour guide," she allowed, giving him a smile that rivaled the dazzling scenery. "I only pray we can get something to nibble on there." A low gurgle of laughter trembled on her lips. "While all this scenic beauty has been ample food for my soul, my stomach is feeling decidedly empty.''

Daring another swift glance at her, Zack was flooded with an aching need to taste her laughing mouth. Lord, how many facets were there to this woman's personality? he wondered, denying himself another look at her by glueing his gaze to the highway. The first time he'd seen her she'd come on like a whirlwind, lighting up the small stage of that club with her vivacity. Then there'd been the subdued, melancholy Aubrey he'd discovered on his bluff, her sparkle dimmed by haunting shadows. The Aubrey who'd toured the gallery had revealed herself as intelligent and knowledgeable, prepared to argue her artistic preferences with him. And now he was faced with a carefree, enthusiastic Aubrey, hungry for the sights, sounds—and taste—of the California Zack loved.

Aubrey was hungry. As he had at lunchtime, Zack felt a thrill of satisfaction. Had he, in some small measure, contributed to the ease of mind that set her appetite free? he mused, loosening his grip on the steering wheel. And, if so, could he then, later, contribute to the freedom of a more basic, earthy hunger? A curl of anticipation unfurled in his midsection as Zack made the turn that would take them into Carmel.

"I want to play tourist." Aubrey made the announcement as she stepped onto the sidewalk that ran along Ocean Avenue, Carmel's main street.

"Okay. I'll tell you what," Zack responded, skimming his gaze up one side of the street then down the other. "Let's amble up this way, then down to the beach on the return trip."

Eagerly falling in with his plan and the stride he'd shortened to accommodate hers, Aubrey slowly paced along the sidewalk, murmuring with delight over the quaint English-style architecture of the shops and the variety of articles offered for sale. But she contented herself with merely window-shopping until they came to a bakery shop. The aroma wafting from the open doorway brought her to an abrupt halt.

"Oh, how heavenly." Closing her eyes, Aubrey inhaled the scent of freshly baked goodies. "I must sample something from this shop," she declared, tugging impatiently on Zack's arm. "Preferably a rich, chewy, nut-filled brownie!"

Smiling indulgently, Zack trailed her into the shop.

"Aren't you afraid you'll ruin your dinner?" he asked moments later, as he strolled beside her, happily munching on the chocolate confection he held in his hand.

"Aren't you?" Aubrey countered, offering him an arch look, while daintily licking a dab of icing from her finger.

"Me?" Zack nearly choked on the word. His lips had become tight and dry from the quickened desire to feel her pink tongue against his skin. Clearing his throat, he continued, "Look at me, woman. A fair amount of food is required to fill up this long frame of mine."

Aubrey was looking, and longing. Startled at her avid response to the sight of him, she firmly directed her gaze to the wide expanse of beach they were approaching. With a shudder of relief, she latched on to an excuse to put distance between them.

Polishing off the last of the sweet, Aubrey slipped out of her shoes and ran down the short incline to the beach.

The white sand was littered with sea vegetation, and as she picked her way through the wet stuff, Aubrey concentrated on the task of bringing her breath under control.

This is ridiculous! she scolded herself, stepping hesitantly into the gently lapping waves. *The man has barely touched you, dammit!* With a muffled yelp, she jumped back. Whether her response was from the chill of the cold water or from shock at her own thoughts, Aubrey didn't know.

Her sudden movement brought her into jarring contact with the long, hard body of the man standing behind her. The sensation of warmth sent skittering through her by Zack's steadying hands was almost as shocking as the splash of the cold ocean water.

"Easy." Zack's breath misted her cheek as he bent low to murmur the word against her ear. "If I hadn't been behind you, you would've found yourself watching the sunset from a prone position." Laughter rippled through his tone. "And getting sand all over that elegant dress in the bargain."

The sunset? Yes! The sunset. Aubrey grasped at the diversion. Breaking free of his loose hold, she sauntered along the white-edged wavelets.

"It's all so beautiful." Aubrey didn't bother to raise her voice above an awed whisper; she was too aware of how closely Zack paced beside her. "And all so very different."

"Different?" Moving nearer, Zack casually draped an arm across her slender shoulders. "From what?"

"From what I'm more accustomed to, of course." Giving in to temptation, Aubrey snuggled into the warmth of his body for, now that the sun was descending, the ocean breeze had cooled and cut through her dress to chill her skin. At least, that's the reasoning she used to grant herself the luxury of burrowing close to him.

"I'm familiar with the New Jersey coastline," she went on to explain. "And though I love it, it's flat, flat, flat in comparison to the cliffs I saw today. In addition, I'm used to seeing the sun rise over the ocean, not set over it."

"You're right." Zack brought her to a halt by applying a gentle squeeze on her upper arm. "I've been to the Jersey coast," he clarified, turning her to face the west. "And though the terrain is vastly different, each has its own particular beauty." Lifting his free arm, he swung it in a sweeping arc. "Just watch and enjoy."

Breath suspended, Aubrey watched as the sun appeared to glide into the Pacific, gilding the undulating blue water with a shimmering coat of first gold, then brass, and then a final, blazing sheen of copper. Her breath trembled from her lips as the sky burst with scarlet before dissolving into deep pink.

"Some show, huh?" Zack's irreverent remark broke the introspective mood creeping over Aubrey. Smiling, she tilted her head to look up into his face.

"Yes, it's a magnificent show," she agreed. "And one I'm glad I didn't miss."

"You don't want to miss that, either." Nodding, Zack turned with her, then pointed at an oddly shaped tree standing sentinel on a promontory jutting out into the sea some distance from where they stood.

"Is that the famous Lone Cypress Tree?"

"The very same." Zack's arm curved again. "And Pebble Beach."

Aubrey's gaze tracked the path his hand gestured toward. "Aren't there a lot of artist types living in this area?"

"Quite a few." Zack nodded as they both turned and began strolling back the way they'd come.

Glancing over her shoulder at the glistening sea, Aubrey sighed. "I'm surprised you didn't settle here."

"I considered it while I was looking at property," Zack admitted. Sliding his arm from her shoulder, he grasped her hand to assist her as they plowed up the incline to the street. "But the minute I saw the bluff, I knew I'd found my place."

Becoming pensive after witnessing the spectacle of sun and sea, Aubrey sighed again. How reassuring to know where you fit in the world, she mused. How secure it must feel to know exactly where you belong. Not since before she'd married Keith had Aubrey enjoyed that reassuring sense of belonging and security.

"Do sunsets always make you dreamy?" Zack's low voice ended her reverie. "We're back at the car."

Starting with surprise, Aubrey glanced around hastily, and laughed shakily as her gaze settled on the Jaguar. "I'm...I'm sorry, Zack. I was in deep thought."

So what else is new? Inexplicably annoyed, Zack clamped his lips together to keep from uttering the retort. As he strode around the car to the driver's side, he reminded himself of his plan to draw Aubrey out of herself. Telling himself that the road to her heart was certainly not paved with sarcasm, he tamped down his irritation and looked questioningly at her.

"On to Monterey?"

Aubrey could feel his anger; it was like a tangible presence separating them. And he had every right to be angry, she thought drearily. No man in his right mind enjoyed the company of an introspective, moody female. Still, she had not been silent all *that* long...had she?

"Did—" Aubrey paused to moisten her dry lips, feeling her breath grow shallow as his eyes followed her action. "Did I miss something?" she finally managed.

"Oh, nothing important." Switching on the engine, Zack cursed himself for his injured tone. "I merely asked if you were ready to go on to dinner."

"Yes, I'm ready." Aubrey tentatively placed her hand on his rigid arm. "I am sorry, Zack," she repeated softly.

Shifting in the seat to face her, Zack felt himself drowning in her imploring eyes. Oh, hell. Why this woman? he mused, lowering his head to her as if drawn by a magnet. Why couldn't he have fallen for a simple, uncomplicated girl, instead of this gorgeous, haunted temptress?

"I'm going to kiss you." Zack thought it fair play to warn her.

"I know." Aubrey waited breathlessly.

"Any objections?"

"Would it matter if there were?"

"Not in the least."

The distance was closed; Zack's mouth brushed hers. *Enough,* he cautioned himself. She isn't ready. Disregarding his own warnings, Zack crushed her lips with his.

The brush of his narrow beard was as soft as a caress! The realization skimmed through Aubrey's mind, then was gone, as was all thought, incinerated by the fire of his mouth. Resistance was beyond her. Response was instinctive and swift. Her hands sought the loosely curled strands of his hair, her fingers trembled as the silk slid against her skin. Her heart thumped painfully at the hesitant touch of his fingers on the outer curve of her breast.

Arching to him, Aubrey sighed and parted her lips in silent invitation.

The invitation was refused.

The lure of the honeyed recess of her sweet mouth brought Zack to his senses. They were in a car parked on a street thronged with tourists, for God's sake! Tearing his mouth from hers, Zack flung his body back into the seat. His hands gripping the steering wheel, he fought to regulate his ragged breathing.

One kiss! he thought in amazement. One short, aborted kiss and he was trembling like a teenager with his first date. He really had it bad!

As his shuddering breath eased to a more normal rate, Zack slanted a glance at the source of his emotional dilemma. Aubrey was obviously as shaken as he was, which offered a small measure of comfort.

"Aubrey, I, ah—" Dammit! Never before had he ever had difficulty expressing his feelings! Railing inwardly, Zack started over. "I wanted to do that very badly," he said, his voice husky. "But not necessarily with an audience of thousands."

Aubrey smiled at his attempt to ease the constraints between them. Lifting her head, she met the warmth in his eyes and shivered. Her lips still burned, her body still trembled. A flippant answer was beyond her capabilities.

"I wanted it, too." In self-defense, she lowered her eyes.

"Dinner." Zack set the car into motion with the abrupt statement. The Jaguar lurched forward. Zack cursed softly as he swerved to avoid grazing a jaywalking tourist.

An unnatural silence prevailed as Zack steered the car through the congested early evening traffic. When he was forced to stop for a red light, he shot a look and a question at her.

"Are you angry?"

Giving up the pretense of gazing out the side window, Aubrey shifted in the seat to face his tight profile. "No, Zack, I'm not angry." Her lips curved appealingly. "Why should I feel angry about being given pleasure?"

Releasing his death grip on the wheel, Zack reached out to test the texture of her cheek with his fingertips. She felt like warm satin, he decided, throwing the car into gear at the impatient sound of a car horn behind them.

When the Jaguar was once again moving smoothly, he tossed a beguiling smile her way.

"Ah, Aubrey," he murmured in a low, sexy tone. "Believe me, the pleasure was all mine."

Aubrey's laughter dispelled the remaining tension. The spirit of camaraderie reestablished, she questioned him eagerly about their destination.

Dusk was settling over the streets of Monterey as Zack parked the car near a large warehouse-type building. The sidewalks were teeming with tourists.

"Cannery Row," Zack said when they'd joined the crowd.

Her face alight with anticipation, Aubrey attempted to look at everything at once. "I want to go in there." She pointed to a large structure with the legend Monterey Canning Company emblazoned on it. "And there." She indicated another building. "And—"

"Then we'd better get started," Zack inserted with a soft chuckle. Clasping her hand in his, he headed for the nearest building she'd indicated. "If you see a restaurant that interests you, sing out," he added, deftly steering her around a group of chattering young people. "The aromas are starting to get to me."

Aubrey knew exactly what he meant. As she inhaled deeply, her mouth began to water at the pervading, distinctive odor of seafood. Following her twitching nose, she made a direct line to the source of the fragrance.

"Will this place do?"

"You have excellent taste," he commented dryly, ushering her into the restaurant.

The atmosphere in the single huge room was one of subdued elegance. The waiters were polite and friendly. The cuisine was delectable. Aubrey consumed every morsel on her plate. At intervals their eyes met over the delicate, wrought-metal lighthouse lamp on the table—Zack's look warm and inviting, Aubrey's gaze wide and wary with shyness.

Declining dessert, they lingered over coffee as Zack recounted the history of Cannery Row. He then went on to tell of its current, flourishing state.

"You know quite a bit about it," Aubrey remarked. "Do you come here often?" She was probing for information about him, even while she wondered at the unusual surge of curiosity she was feeling.

"On and off." Zack shrugged. "I own an old warehouse here."

"A warehouse!" Aubrey laughed in amazement. "Whatever for? Are you a merchant as well as a sculptor?"

Zack was shaking his head before she'd finished speaking. "No, Aubrey, I'm not a merchant. My studio at the complex is too small for the large pieces I occasionally do. I work on the bigger projects in the warehouse."

Suddenly Aubrey felt awkward and gauche. Never once had she wondered where his more imposing artworks were created. A vision of the sculpture on display in the complex's courtyard flashed into her mind. "Did you do your *Sunset* here in Monterey?"

"Yes." Settling the check, Zack smiled gently as he escorted her from the restaurant. When they were once again on the sidewalk, he tilted his head inquiringly. "Would you like to see my warehouse?"

"I'd love to!" Aubrey exclaimed. "Is it far from here?"

"Some distance beyond the marina." He shrugged. "We'll take the car, then stop at Fisherman's Wharf before heading back down the coast."

Though the warehouse was old it was in excellent condition. The echo of their footsteps reverberated loudly through the spacious building. Cold waves rose from the cement floor, permeating the still air.

"You work in here alone?" Glancing around with interest, Aubrey examined the "tools" of Zack's trade. Somewhat amazed, she identified molds of varying sizes, industrial equipment, such as an electric arc and gas welding tools, and a confusing assortment of wire, piping, sheet metal and even what looked to her like piles of junk metal.

"All alone." Amusement laced his quiet tone. "I'm an artiste, you know." His voice changed dramatically. "We artistes require solitude."

He was laughing at himself! Zack was not merely teasing her, Aubrey realized, he was poking fun at himself. Laughing with him, Aubrey added the word *unaffected* to her steadily growing list of adjectives describing him.

Smiling with him, Aubrey indicated the variety of materials with a vague hand motion. "How do you use all this, ah, stuff?" she asked brightly.

"In different ways, depending on the size of the piece I happen to be working on," Zack answered seriously. "To make an armature, or framework, I use wire for smaller pieces and metal tubing for larger works. Some of my figures require casting, which I'm equipped to do right here. Others I work by hand."

"I see." Aubrey really didn't comprehend fully, but she got the drift . . . she hoped. Her brows arched as her gaze came to rest on a long table. "And how do you use those?" she asked, her glance skipping over an assortment of power saws, drills and hammers.

"The tools are used by a sculptor for the assemblage technique." He shrugged and grinned. "Which simply means a piece of work created by assembling ready-made materials." His grin faded to a wry smile. "Look, this has to be boring as hell for you—"

"Not at all!" Aubrey cut in insistently, unsuccessfully containing a shiver.

"Liar." Walking to her, Zack curved an arm around her shoulders to draw her close to his own body warmth. "Besides which, you're freezing." Ignoring her sputtered protest, he urged her toward the door. "Come on," he coaxed, "I'll buy you a drink on Fisherman's Wharf."

Six

___

Zack hadn't kissed her good-night.

Shoulders slumped, Aubrey stood at the window in her motel room staring into space. During the drive back from Monterey she'd tingled in anticipation of a reenactment of the searing kiss they'd shared in the car in Carmel.

Why hadn't he kissed her good-night?

Sighing, Aubrey rested her forehead against the cool pane. She had enjoyed the day so very much. From breakfast straight through the snack they'd indulged in on Fisherman's

Wharf, the entire day had been perfect. All it had lacked was a lingering good-night kiss. Aubrey imagined she could still taste their twilight kiss.

Zack. A shiver trickled down Aubrey's spine. What a genuinely nice man Zackery Sharp was.

Nice? Aubrey moved her head back and forth on the glass. Zackery Sharp was much, much more than nice. Zack had a veritable multitude of facets—some seemingly in conflict. Aubrey smiled. Zack was arrogant and humble, even though he disclaimed the latter. He was, in turn, charming and abrasive, carefree and somber, considerate and thoughtless, sharing and selfish and altogether, completely, totally sexy.

Sexy. The shiver along Aubrey's spine intensified. She had felt the lure of Zack's attraction countless times during the wonderful hours they'd spent together. A whimsical smile touched her lips fleetingly. She hadn't been alone in her appreciation of his masculine appeal, either. She had noticed the speculative gleam of interest in the feminine glances cast his way in Carmel and Monterey. The flashes of jealousy aroused in her by the avid, measuring looks had shaken Aubrey to the core.

Now, alone with her jumbled emotions and thoughts, Aubrey was very much afraid that one of those emotions was edging perilously close to love for the tall man. And love was the one emotion she didn't want to experience.

But, God, she had wanted him—all of him—almost desperately while his mouth was devouring hers.

Feeling the shiver change to the heat of shame, Aubrey shook her head despairingly. Never before had she felt such an overwhelming physical need, not even in the early days of her marriage to Keith. To Aubrey, longing for Zack's possession seemed like a betrayal of the vows she'd taken with her husband and, in a way she couldn't even define, like a betrayal of the child she and Keith had created without love—the child lost because of pride.

A tormented moan whispered through Aubrey's lips. Right or wrong, she wanted Zack, even knowing it could never be. Zack was a fine man.

But the bottom line was that Aubrey Mason was simply not good enough for Zackery Sharp. If nothing else, Zack deserved a free spirited woman; Aubrey Mason was shackled by memories.

Aubrey closed her eyes against the sting of tears, and immediately opened them again at the distant rumble of thunder. A few moments later, the sky was illuminated by a flash of lightning, revealing massing storm clouds roiling inland from the sea. She winced at a second, closer bolt of lightning. Without conscious thought or direction, she was moving. Flinging the door open, she ran into the rising wind.

Zack couldn't sleep. Finally giving up the pretense, he pushed back the sheet and rolled off the bed. Idly rubbing a hand over his naked chest, he strolled to the windows that looked out over the courtyard. Pushed by the force of wind, the rain danced fanatically across the flagstone yard. A long, crackling finger of lightning streaked through the sky, momentarily bathing the copper statue in an eerie light.

Did storms bother Aubrey? Zack frowned at the thought. She had lost her family in a storm. And now she was alone in a strange motel room, and it was storming.

Should he go to her? Uncertainty held Zack motionless. Would Aubrey feel indignant or reassured if he went to her offering the haven of his arms?

Turning from the window, Zack grabbed up the slacks he'd tossed over a chair. Aubrey was getting company whether she wanted it or not. Sliding his feet into leather thongs, he strode from the bedroom, pulling a shirt on as he headed for the door.

There was another, brighter flash of lightning as he passed the living room windows. For an instant the night was as day.

"What the hell!"

Zack came to an abrupt halt. In that brief moment of clarity he could have sworn he'd caught a glimpse of someone out there on the bluff.

Naw; Zack shook his head. No one with half a brain would expose himself or herself to the driving wind and rain whipping over the land. He was wasting time.

Zack was on the point of pivoting away when another brilliant bolt of lightning streaked through the clouds. In the luminous glow, he recognized her at once. She was kneeling in the exact position as the day before, her black mane swirling madly in the wind.

"Dammit!"

Emotions boiled inside Zack—feelings of compassion, anger, protectiveness propelled him to the outside door. What was he letting himself in for? Zack shrugged off the question as he hurtled down the stairs. Aubrey needed him. He took the last three steps in a leap. Hell, it was beginning to look as though Aubrey needed a full-time keeper! Zack mentally appointed himself to the job as he dashed through the rain.

Zack didn't say anything as he came up beside Aubrey; he was too angry to say anything. His movements fluid, he bent to lift her. After scooping her up in his arms, he dashed back to the house.

"Zack! What do you—" Aubrey began on a gasped breath.

"Shut up!" Zack snarled at her. "And be still," he commanded when she started to wriggle, "or I might decide to pitch you into the sea." Sheer fury pumped adrenaline into his veins. His breathing barely ruffled, he charged up the stairs and through the door he'd left standing wide open.

"Are you nuts?" Zack punctuated the question by slamming the door shut with a vicious backward kick.

Aubrey was soaking wet; they were both soaking wet. Rain ran off their bodies to puddle on the living room carpet as Zack glared down into her glistening face.

"No!" The denial sprang from her lips. "Zack, you have no ri—"

"What the hell did you think you were doing out there?" Zack tightened his arms when she began to struggle. "Be still and answer me."

"Zack, your carpet!" Aubrey exclaimed belatedly.

"To hell with the carpet!" Zack was nearly shouting. "The carpet can be replaced—you can't."

"I can be replaced by almost anyone!" Aubrey shouted back at him. "Don't you understand? I'm empty—there's nothing left inside. What there was of me drowned off that damned island. I have nothing to offer."

Instead of giving him pause, her words added fuel to the angry fire blazing in Zack. Grief he could understand and deal with. But futility was beyond his comprehension; life was too sweet to dismiss without a fight. Zack *did* understand and appreciate a good fight.

"You're wrong, Aubrey. You've a great deal to offer." Zack's voice, though pitched lower, still vibrated from the fury racing through him. "You're a talented performer, you're intelligent, you're energetic and..." His voice faded as a shiver trembled down her body. "And you're freezing!"

"I'm all right," Aubrey muttered.

"You're not all right, dammit!" More incensed than ever, Zack raked her body with a steely-eyed glance. She had changed into jeans, a baggy sweatshirt and sneakers, all of which were sodden and heavy with water. "Kick off your sneakers," he bit out tersely, stepping out of the now-slippery leather thongs. "Now!" he snapped when she didn't comply.

The muddy sneakers dropped to the floor with a squishy plop. Zack didn't hear the foot gear land. He was already crossing the living room with Aubrey in his arms, heading for the bathroom off the guest room. Setting her feet on the carpeted floor, he began tugging the sweatshirt off her shivering body.

"Zack!" Aubrey made a fruitless attempt to step away from him. "I can do it!"

Zack didn't bother to reply. With a final yank, he pulled the dripping shirt up and over her head and tossed it into the bathtub. Aubrey was not wearing a bra. Her nipples were puckered from the brush of the cold, wet material. Zack barely noticed—his fingers were already busy working on the snap closure of her jeans.

The sodden denim clung to Aubrey's legs. Muttering a curse, Zack dropped to one knee to ease the material away from her cold skin.

"Zack, please!" Aubrey protested, her face hot in contrast to the rest of her chilled body.

"Be still." Fighting the jeans, Zack pulled and tugged until they pooled around her slender ankles. "Step out of them." His harsh voice held an underlying thickness; the fact that she was now completely undressed had finally filtered through the anger burning inside him. Suddenly Zack was burning for a different reason. His chest tightened as he slowly raised his eyes.

Cooled by the wind and rain, Aubrey's skin gleamed with a pale translucence. Zack's breath grew constrained as he slowly absorbed the delicate curve of her calves, the strong, supple length of her thighs, the womanly roundness of her hips, the tucked-in neatness of her waist, her small, perfectly molded breasts, the inviting slope of her shoulders and her soft, trembling lips. He could barely breathe at all by the time his gaze came to rest on her wide violet eyes.

"Aubrey." Her name whispered through his dry lips as he stood to his full height. His eyes were darkened to near black. His need was great. All memory of his plan to cautiously bring her out of despair was burned to ashes by the fire blazing out of control in every cell of his body.

"No." Aubrey's murmured denial lacked conviction. She was so very warm, so very aware of Zack's utter masculinity, her own femininity. A strange weakness swept through her as she helplessly watched him remove his own wet clothes. As the evidence of his arousal was revealed to her, she moved her head restlessly from side to side. She didn't even feel the icy drops of water that were flung from the dripping strands of her hair onto her back and shoulders.

Zack didn't say anything. But then, there really wasn't anything to say. The heat of desire blazing from his eyes, the melting acceptance shimmering in hers, said it all. His hands touched her waist, slid around to her back and then he pulled her into his arms, a strangled groan vibrating in his throat.

Unmindful of the moisture dripping off their hair, the dampness of their bodies, Zack lifted Aubrey off her feet and carried her along the short hall to the room he kept ready for his sister. The lavender-draped single bed was tiny in comparison to the custom-made king in his own room. Zack didn't notice.

Driven by a consuming need unlike anything he'd ever felt before, Zack placed Aubrey in the center of the narrow bed, his gaze locked on her passion-clouded eyes.

"I won't be gentle." A twinge of conscience forced the admittance from him.

"I know." Aubrey's small breasts rose and fell with each ragged breath. Empty, denied the fulfillment of masculine power for over three years, her body writhed, arching in a demand for his.

The time for words was long past. Growling an inarticulate mutter that might have been her name, Zack covered her pale body with the hard golden beauty of his own.

There was no hesitation, no holding back. The voracious hunger clawing at him shattered what little control he had left as Zack made them complete with one swift, desperate thrust.

A low cry of joy was wrenched from Aubrey's throat at his piercing possession. Exquisite pleasure radiated through her being. Head thrown back, throat arched, she released all inhibition, responding wildly to the intensity of Zack's fierce, primitive rhythm.

"Yes, yes," he groaned encouragingly as she clasped her arms and legs around him in a lover's embrace. "Give to me. Take from me."

His pace increased as Zack drove himself relentlessly to be one with her. Sensation after sensation, each more excruciatingly sweet than the last, shuddered the length of his body, driving him on toward the goal of perfect communion.

Aubrey's chest and throat were tight. Her stomach muscles clenched. Every nerve and sinew in her body tensed in preparation for long-denied release. Her nails dug into Zack's flesh as she hovered an instant on the edge, then his name was torn from her aching throat in a muted scream as wave after wave of pleasure washed over her. Vaguely, as if from a great distance, Aubrey heard Zack's hoarse cry of triumph and felt the pulsation of his life force.

Reality returned with the sensation of cold clamminess. Drawing an uneven, steadying breath, Aubrey unlocked the grip her fingers maintained on Zack's muscular shoulders. Uncertain now, she pressed her fingers gently against his skin.

Passion spent, Zack desired nothing more than to remain buried deeply within Aubrey's satiny warmth. At the hesitant press of her fingers, he reluctantly raised his head from her scented shoulder to stare into her violet eyes.

"Am I crushing you?" Zack's tone was rich from the afterglow of lovemaking.

"No." Aubrey moved her head on the spread, grimacing at the brush of sodden cold against her rapidly cooling skin. "I...I'm cold. The bed's soaked from my wet hair."

Zack frowned and shifted his heavy-lidded gaze to the lavender covering. His eyes widened as he caught sight of the saturated area around her head. Using his arms as levers, he lifted his body from hers.

"I've got to get you dry and warm." Propelled into action, he leaped from the bed and strode to a closet. "Up, Aubrey," he said, plunging a hand into the closet to retrieve a terry robe and a small blow dryer. Striding back to her, he handed her the robe and dropped the dryer onto the bed. "While you're drying your hair, I'll get you a hot drink." Not waiting for a response, he strode out of the room.

Gratefully slipping into the warmth of the lavender-colored robe, Aubrey tried to deny the curl of jealousy that unwound inside her. Whose robe was she wearing? It was obviously a woman's. As she glanced around she noticed that the room was obviously a woman's bedroom. Did Zack keep it to accommodate a frequent female visitor?

Glancing down at the bed, Aubrey winced as she pictured Zack and a faceless woman, their bodies entwined. A low protesting gasp clogged her throat. Tearing her gaze from the bed, she walked to the dresser. After plugging the dryer into a wall socket, she directed the hot air at her hair, and her gaze to the wall mirror.

Whoever she was, the woman was taller than Aubrey. The midthigh-length robe hung to below her knees and the sleeves would have covered her hands if she hadn't rolled them up. Aubrey was suddenly disdainful of tall women. Telling herself that Zack's love life was none of her business, she ruthlessly applied the brush she'd found on the dresser top to her tangled, damp mane. She was smoothing the nearly dry strands into order when Zack called to her from the living room.

"Coffee's ready, Aubrey. Are you almost finished?"

A distant flare of light drew Aubrey's gaze to the window. Through the tempest created between them, she'd forgotten the storm. Had Zack likewise forgotten his anger at discovering her outside in the rain? Unplugging the dryer, she squared her shoulders as she turned and walked to the doorway.

What she chose to do was really none of Zack's business, she assured herself bracingly, just as his love life was none of hers. However, Aubrey's heart began to race as she approached the living room from the short hallway.

Aubrey didn't make it into the living room. Zack caught her around the arm as she stepped out of the hall.

"Come with me," he murmured, drawing her toward another room at the end of the hallway. "I have a fire going in the fireplace in my bedroom." His tread firm, Zack left her with little choice but to move with him. Nevertheless, Aubrey resisted—at least verbally.

"No, Zack. I really should go back to the motel."

He didn't reply until he'd drawn her into the spacious, dimly lit room. "No, you really should not," he contradicted her blandly, guiding her to a large circular rattan chair he'd moved close to the crackling fire. Gently but firmly he seated her on the deeply piled velvet cushion nestled in the cone-shaped chair. Dropping lazily into a matching chair opposite her, Zack smiled as he handed her a steaming mug of coffee.

"You're tired," he said softly. "I'm tired." A hint of wryness quirked his lips. "It's been a long day, ending with a traumatic night. We both need sleep."

Aubrey could hardly argue with that statement. She felt drained, physically and emotionally. She didn't want to talk. Most of all she didn't want to think; thinking hurt. Sipping the hot coffee, she eyed him warily over the rim of the cup. She nearly choked on the hot brew when he so very calmly relayed his plans for them both.

"We also need to talk," Zack went on quietly. "But that can wait till tomorrow morning. What we're going to do is finish our coffee and go to bed." He jerked his head to indicate the enormous bed behind him.

"Zack!" Aubrey had to clutch the mug to prevent it from falling from her trembling fingers.

"Once in bed," Zack continued unperturbed by her outburst, "we are going to make slow, satisfying love. And then we're both going to sleep the clock around."

The heat that suffused Aubrey's body had nothing to do with the flames leaping in the fireplace. Excitement danced a crazy jig along her nervous system. The smoldering expression on Zack's face as he set his mug aside and moved to stand before her, arms extended in invitation, caused an ache in the lower part of Aubrey's body that was shocking in its intensity.

Not a murmur of protest passed her lips as he removed the mug from her nerveless fingers, or when he lifted her up into his arms and carried her to the bed. Not until he tugged to loosen the tie belt on the robe did she attempt to forestall him.

"Who...whose robe is this?" she gulped as he pushed the soft material from her shoulders.

"Kit keeps it here for when she visits," Zack replied, distractedly.

"Kit?" Aubrey gasped as his own robe was cast aside to join hers on the floor.

"Yes, Kit." Sliding onto the bed beside her, Zack frowned. "My sister. Didn't I mention her to you?"

"Oh!" Aubrey shivered as one long hand captured one achingly aroused breast. "No," she puffed, "I don't think so."

"Sorry." Zack's breathing grew uneven as he stroked her silky skin. "Remind me to tell you about her sometime." Bending to her, he parted his lips. "God, Aubrey, give me your mouth."

Aubrey surrendered without a whimper. As her eyes closed, her lips parted to join with his. With gentle sweetness, Zack's mouth explored the textures and contours of hers. With infinite care, he dipped his tongue into the honeyed recess of her mouth. Every caress, every stroke of his hands aroused a delicious shiver from her, every successive, harder kiss drew a moan from deep within her throat.

Zack's lovemaking was slow and easy and blatantly erotic. Aubrey was whispering his name in an enticing plea for unity when at last he moved to cover her pliant softness with his rock-hard body. A long, ragged breath whispered from her throat at the sensuous feel of his hair-roughened thighs brushing the silkiness of hers.

"Zack . . . please." Aubrey's voice was little more than a broken sob.

"How should I please you, my love?" he murmured, drawing a line of fire down the arched column of her throat with the tip of his tongue.

"Give me your flame," she begged. "Fill the emptiness inside me with it."

"Yes, yes, I'm a flame," he groaned, seeking her lips with his hungry mouth. "A flame you've ignited." Grasping her hands, he laced their fingers together, then slowly slid their bound arms straight out to either side of their bodies. "And a flame only you can extinguish." He moved his hips sensuously against her. Instinctively, Aubrey arched her body in readiness for his. "Envelop your flame, my love."

Aubrey shuddered with pleasure as Zack slowly lit the emptiness with his flame.

Sleep had eluded Zack. Standing with his back to the window, hands jammed into the pockets of his robe, he stared broodingly at the delicate woman curled up under the covers on his bed.

In sleep, Aubrey was even more heart-wrenchingly beautiful than ever. The flush of richly satisfying lovemaking tinged her normally pale skin. Her long, thick eyelashes fanned her sleep-softened cheeks. Her glorious black mane was spread out on the pillow like a shimmering halo. Her lips curved with gentle appeal.

Zack hurt with love for her. A sigh expanded his broad chest. He hurt for himself, as well.

His beautiful, elusive Aubrey had used him. A bittersweet smile touched Zack's lips. Wasn't it usually the woman who made the accusation of being used? The traditional role switch was ironic and almost amusing.

Zack wasn't laughing. He wasn't sleeping, either. Exhaling harshly, he stared longingly at the woman lost to the world's reality in slumber. What was Aubrey's reality? As if in answer, an echo of her angry voice rang inside Zack's head.

"I can be replaced by almost anyone! Don't you understand? I'm empty—there's nothing left inside. What there was of me drowned off that damned island. I have nothing to offer.

"I'm empty."

Zack shivered inside the warm robe as the echo relentlessly continued.

"Give me your flame. Fill the emptiness inside me."

A stinging sickness filled Zack's throat. In the intense heat of that moment he had actually believed that it was *him*, his possession, Aubrey craved. What an arrogant fool he was.

The sensation that washed over Zack was too close to agony to be tolerated. Hating the pain, Zack turned his back on the cause of it. His attempt at escape was unsuccessful.

The pearlized light of predawn bathed the statue of the kneeling woman in a muted copper glow. Reaching toward the sun, the gleaming inanimate arms were evocative of the pale, vibrantly alive arms that had clung so sweetly to him.

Zack's fingers curled into his palms. Breathing heavily, he fought down the urge to take a hammer to his most prized creation. In that instant, Zack acknowledged the reason for his refusal to sell the statue. The shining copper woman was a solid representation of all he sought for in a lifetime mate. In the most basic terms, Zack knew he had refused to part with the copper kneeling woman because he loved it.

His movements uncharacteristically uncoordinated, Zack spun away from the window to walk to the foot of the huge bed. In his mind the two were as one: the inanimate and the living, the still and the quick. Aubrey was the embodiment of the kneeling woman.

A sad smile pulled at Zack's lips. Had fate played the most cruel of tricks on him? Had he found the living prototype of his copper woman, only to discover that she was as devoid of life as the statue?

"I'm empty—there's nothing left inside."

Aubrey's cry, and yet she had cried out again during the throes of passion.

"Give me your flame. Fill the emptiness inside me."

Zack closed his eyes as the pain expanded in his chest. Was lovemaking Aubrey's touchstone to reality? he mused. Did she use the act of physical contact with a man to assure herself of her own life? Had she used *him* for the purpose of reaffirming her own existence?

Zack fervently prayed that he was wrong, but he was very much afraid that he was right. For a moment, utter defeat lay on his shoulders and his eyes grew dull with futility. Then slowly Zack lifted his chin and the light of challenge brightened his eyes.

No! He would be damned before he'd allow her to dismiss her own value, and his own expectations, so recklessly. Now that he'd found her, he was not about to step aside while she wandered down the road to a futile existence.

Suddenly exhausted, Zack pulled at the tie belt on his robe as he circled around to the side of the bed.

Dropping the robe to the floor, he slid into the bed. Not for a second did he allow himself to believe that drawing Aubrey from her world of shadows into the light would be a simple matter. What he *had* to believe was that he could do it.

Carefully slipping his arms around her waist, he drew her to him, spoonfashion. Murmuring incoherently, Aubrey snuggled into his warmth.

"Zack?"

A tender smile curved Zack's lips at the fuzzy sound of her voice. "Yes," he whispered, rubbing his cheek over her silky hair.

"Why aren't you asleep?" Though Aubrey's words ran together, Zack understood the question.

"I've been wondering about something." His arms tightened as though in fear of her escape. "Aubrey, why were you out there on the bluff in that storm?" Feeling his throat thicken, Zack rushed on softly, "Were you considering a, ah, permanent solution to end your emptiness?" The instant he'd finished speaking, Zack drew in a deep breath and held it. Fortunately Aubrey's response was reassuringly prompt.

"Permanent . . . ?" she repeated in a confused tone. Then enlightenment struck and she stiffened. "No!" Aubrey's vehement denial disspelled doubt. "I would never—ever—consider such an answer to *any* problem!"

The pent-up breath shivered from Zack in a sigh of relief. Nuzzling his face into her hair, he stroked his palm soothingly over her hip and down her thigh, relaxing as he felt the tension ease out of her body.

"You must believe that, Zack," Aubrey pleaded in a hushed, aching tone.

"I do believe you, sweetheart." Zack's voice was rough with emotion. "Go back to sleep now. I'm sorry I upset you."

Zack felt Aubrey's body relax, then heard the soft sigh preceding sleep. Inhaling slowly, he closed his eyes and drifted into a half sleep. At least that was one problem he no longer had to deal with, he decided, yawning widely. They'd have a long talk, or even a confrontation if necessary... tomorrow.

Some five hours later, Zack was jarred awake by a persistent pounding on the door. Sitting bolt upright, he glanced around. Aubrey was not in the bed. A towel wrapped around her slender body, she came into the room from the connecting bath as he opened his mouth to call for her.

"Zack, where are my clothes?" She raked a hand through her hair. "I've got to dress. There's someone at the door."

Already out of the bed and shrugging into his robe, Zack suppressed a sigh of relief at the sight of her while indicating the kitchen with a distracted gesture.

"Your clothes are in the dryer, in the room behind the kitchen." Zack frowned as another, sharper rap was applied to the door. "Dammit! I've got to find out who the hell's trying to break down the door." He was talking to himself; Aubrey had already dashed for the laundry room.

So much for his plans for an in-depth discussion with Aubrey, Zack grumbled to himself, striding across the living room. He began cursing when there was another hard rap against the wood. Silently promising severe bruising, if not outright dismemberment, to the persistent intruder, Zack grasped the knob and angrily flung the door open. The sight that met his eyes shocked him into absolute immobility. For one wild instant, Zack had the weird sensation that while he'd slept, someone had erected a full-length mirror outside his door.

Seven

"Hello, yourself."

The drawl was pure West Texas, the grin was a mirror image of Zack's own.

"Thackery?" Stunned, Zack just stood there.

The tall, mustached reflection raised one burnished brow and nodded sharply. "There's somebody else running around with this face we share?" he asked dryly. Then, not waiting for a response, he continued, "I was invited. May we come in?"

"Yes! Yes, of course." Prodded out of confusion by his brother's voice, Zack stepped back. As he swung the door open, he noticed the other person comprised in the "we" of the request. The woman by Thackery's side was beautiful. Above average in height, she was elegantly slender, with classic features and shoulder-length auburn hair. As the couple moved into the room, Zack belatedly extended his hand.

"Damn, Thackery, I can't tell you how delighted I am to finally meet you." The hand that grasped Zack's was hard and callused.

"The name's Thack, and the feeling's mutual." Thack's smile softened his sun and wind-roughened face. His eyes took on a tender glow as he glanced at the woman standing patiently beside him. "And this is my wife, Barbara."

Aubrey heard the end of the introduction as she came out of the kitchen. As Zack had moments before, she stopped dead, her startled gaze shifting back and forth between the identical men.

Good heavens! she thought in amazement. The resemblance was uncanny! From a distance, Aubrey felt sure that had it not been for the narrow beard on the one, and the mustache on the other, she wouldn't have known which twin was which. Incredible!

"Ah, Aubrey," Zack held out his hand in invitation. "Come meet my brother and sister-in-law."

While dressing, Aubrey's stomach had churned sickeningly at the thought of facing Zack. What, she'd wondered, must he be thinking of her now, after the night they'd spent together? She had given herself to him so completely, with such wild abandon that the mere thought of it made her face flame. Had Zack concluded that she lavished herself in that way on a number of men? she'd fretted. More important, would he make demands on her that she couldn't possibly fulfill?

Now, as she crossed the room to him, all her fears of a scene between them were banished by the compassionate warmth that spread through her. After all these years, Zack was standing close to the brother he had thought was lost to him. Even loving Zack against her will, Aubrey shared his happiness.

Up close, Aubrey was able to discern the shadings of differences between the brothers. All the while the attractive couple were being presented to her, and she to them, Aubrey scrutinized the two male visages, noting the similarities as well as the differences.

While they were of equal height and build, Thack's body had a raw-boned, rangy muscularity in contrast to Zack's sleek, well-conditioned slenderness. They shared the same golden skin tone, but even there the hues varied from Thack's weathered, dull burnish to Zack's California sun-kissed bronze. Though the same white-gold in color, their hair was worn in different styles; Thack's unruly loose curls appeared to have a will of their own and caressed the back of his neck, whereas Zack's had been trimmed to behave more decorously. Whereas Thack had the toughened look of well-tanned leather, Zack had the cool appearance of tempered steel. Standing side by side, the brothers Sharp presented a formidable picture.

On close inspection, Aubrey discovered the single feature that was absolutely alike. Both Zack and Thack looked out on the world through brown eyes that revealed shrewd intelligence and tolerant humor. Loving the one brother, Aubrey couldn't help but feel an immediate closeness to the other.

Standing with his arm draped casually over Aubrey's shoulders, grinning like a boy given an unexpected treat, Zack was the first person to realize that they *were* simply standing there.

"Good Lord!" he exclaimed, shaking his head. "Come in and sit down, make yourselves comfortable." He started to move into the living room, then paused to glance hesitantly at Thack. "You were planning to stay awhile?"

Aubrey felt a twinge of empathy for the anxious thread woven through Zack's congenial tone. Slanting a glance at Thack, she felt the twinge give way to a glow as the uncertain smile on his lips eased to a relaxed grin.

"We had thought to visit for a spell." Thack shifted his gaze to his wife. "Barb and I are still officially on our honeymoon."

Zack halted in his tracks. "You were married recently?"

"Yes," Barbara answered softly.

"One week, three days and—" Thack shot a glance at his watch "—two and a half hours ago exactly." His eyes danced with deviltry. "And I'm not even tired of her yet."

This time the twinge pierced a little deeper into Aubrey's chest as she joined Zack in wishing the couple congratulations and happiness. Why she should experience even the tiniest shaft of pain unnerved Aubrey. Surely the twinge of emotion was in no way related to envy. Of course not, Aubrey assured herself. The absolute last thing she was looking for was a commitment...with Zack or any other man. She was merely suffering morning-after pangs of depression, that's all.

Latching on to the rationale, Aubrey forced a brilliant smile to her lips and turned her attention to Zack, who was in the process of issuing an invitation.

"And I'll order something sent up from the restaurant," he was saying. "How does that sound?"

"Sounds fine to me." Thack grinned. "I was about to suggest we amble down to the restaurant. But I'd just as soon stay here. I'm a kitchen sitter myself." He cocked his head at Barbara. "What do you think, honey?"

Barbara smiled indulgently at Thack before addressing Zack. "I think that would be lovely, Zack." Her lips twitched, then her smile turned into outright laughter. "Zackery and Thackery! I still can't believe it!"

Leading his wife into the dining room, Thack gave Zack a look of long suffering. "You'll have to forgive Barb, Zack," he said dryly. "She sure has gotten one hellava lot of laugh miles out of our names."

Just then, Zack turned to slide a chair away from the table for Aubrey and noticed that she, too, was making a valiant effort to contain her laughter.

"It appears that the condition is contagious," he observed, unsuccessfully fighting a grin. "But you must admit, the combination of names *does* have amusement value."

"Like Frick and Frack?" Thack rejoined.

"Or tic and tac?" Barbara giggled.

"And crick and crack?" Aubrey gasped.

"Oh, my aching back," Zack muttered, heading for the kitchen. "Coffee. I'm surrounded by clowns and I haven't even had my first cup of coffee yet."

The nonsense dispersed whatever reserve remained from the initial meeting. While waiting for the food to be sent up from the restaurant below, the two couples sat around the dining room table, drinking the coffee Zack had brewed and generally getting to know one another.

Two large bottles accompanied the meal when it arrived. The imported champagne went a long way in easing the atmosphere and loosening tongues. Unused to wine so early in the day, Aubrey was feeling both mellow and drowsy by the time Zack topped off her glass for the third time.

Lazing back in the padded rattan chair, she was content to simply listen as her lover and his brother caught up with each other's life.

"I had no idea I was related to such a famous person."

Her eyes cloudy with memories of the night before, Aubrey let her gaze linger on Zack's face, and never even heard the response he made to Thack's comment.

"And now you've given up being a lawman to become a full-time rancher?"

Zack's question pierced the fog, and Aubrey frowned. "Lawman?" she repeated.

Zack peered at her closely, then laughed. "I think you're either half asleep or half sloshed, Aubrey. Thack's just told me he recently retired from the Texas Rangers."

"Oh." Aubrey blinked owlishly, and added airily, "Please, do continue."

Though the others laughed softly, it was an understanding laugh, without malice. Aubrey laughed with them. When the conversation resumed, she settled back in the cozy chair and drifted away again, soothed by the feelings of warmth and belonging seeping through her.

It had been years—exactly three years— since Aubrey had allowed herself this sense of comforting ease and relaxation with other people. Slowly, as the effects of rigorous love-making, too little sleep and too much wine took their toll, her eyelids lost the battle with the weights that seemed to be tugging at them.

Floating in the realm between wakefulness and sleep, Aubrey heard the conversation swirl around her while not a word of it registered. Though the voices were muted by her wine-induced haze, Zack's distinct tones filtered through to lull her senses.

Zack. Aubrey shivered delicately. Even though she was half asleep, the mere thought of him aroused a response in her heart and her flesh. Never, not even in her wildest, teenage dreams, had she imagined the possibility of the beauty and power she'd discovered in his arms. Nor had she believed herself sensually capable of such responsive abandonment.

Heat radiated through Aubrey, heat generated by the memory of their lovemaking, and it had been *lovemaking*, not merely the casual giving and taking she'd experienced with her husband. But then, she had never been in love with Keith, had never imagined she could fall in love so quickly or as deeply as she now loved Zack.

And it was all so hopeless.

The stark realization pierced the sleepy, sensual mist clouding Aubrey's mind. She understood hopelessness; she'd lived with it for three long years. If she'd learned nothing else, she'd learned there were no happily-ever-afters, at least not for her.

Soft, feminine laughter drew Aubrey's attention. Looking up, she observed the animated expression on Barbara's face as she gazed at her lounging husband. Near adoration was shining out of Barbara's hazel eyes. That Thack returned his wife's feeling was blatantly obvious.

This time, Aubrey wearily admitted to the searing twinge of envy that twisted inside her chest. And with the admission, she knew she had to get away from Zack for a while. She had to be by herself. She had to think clearly, and thinking while Zack was around was proving to be an impossibility.

Schooling her expression into polite interest, Aubrey tuned back into the conversation—and immediately wished she hadn't. Male pride gleaming in his dark eyes, Thack was relating to Zack how Barbara had thrown over the opportunity to be a top model to be with him.

"It was not a major decision, Thack," Barbara inserted softly, downplaying the importance of her career.

"Not major!" Thack exclaimed. "Do you hear the woman?" he demanded of Zack. "After years of hard work and marginal success, she could have had it all." Thack's expression revealed the wonder he was still feeling. "She turned her back on it for an accident-prone rancher she had known for a week." Thack shook his head. "Can you believe it?"

"Yes," Zack replied quietly. "The woman's obviously in love."

"Yeah." Thack's grin lit his face. "And the woman is loved."

Barbara's face bloomed with pleasurable color. Aubrey's cheeks paled. She could feel

Zack's compelling gaze and refused to meet it. She suddenly felt uncomfortable with the unselfconscious love Thack and Barbara shared. And the last thing she wanted was to look into Zack's eyes and see a reflection of that love. As beautiful and as satisfying as their shared passion had been, it had been only that—passion shared. Zack was not in love with her, Aubrey assured herself. He could not be in love with her. She just couldn't bear it if he was.

Fighting the sense of panic that was building within her, Aubrey pushed her chair back and stood up. Three pairs of questioning eyes observed her action.

"Aubrey?" Zack murmured.

"I, ah, I thought I'd clear these dishes away." Aubrey smiled faintly. "It's midafternoon already. I—I have some things I must do. I must go back to the motel room." Belatedly, Aubrey remembered tearing out of her room the night before and leaving the door unlocked.

"Yeah, we'd better get a move on, too, honey." Thack smiled at Barbara. "I only hope they have a vacancy in that motel across the road."

Zack had been frowning at Aubrey, but with Thack's words, he turned to his brother. "You haven't registered?"

Thack shook his head. "No. We came right here."

"And you'll stay right here." Zack paused, then asked, "Unless you'd rather be alone?"

Here? Now Aubrey frowned as she pictured the single bed in the guest room, and ran her gaze over Thack's long frame as he got to his feet. Where...

Zack answered the question as it was forming in her mind. "Even though you'd have all the privacy you could want. The guest room's on the other side of the living room and it has its own bath."

"What do you think, honey?" Thack glanced down at Barbara.

"I'd love to stay," Barbara said simply. "This is a beautiful place."

"Good," Zack declared.

Good, Aubrey seconded silently, thinking there could hardly be a replay of the night before with Zack's brother and his wife in the apartment.

"Okay, let's get this mess cleared away." Zack's tone was light with satisfaction. "Then we'll get you two settled in."

With the four of them working, the lunch debris was cleaned up in minutes. The kitchen and dining room restored to order, Zack herded Aubrey, Barbara and Thack along the hallway that continued on the far side of his bedroom.

"Your room is back here," he told Thack, motioning to a door to his right. "And this—" he gestured to a door to his left "—is an elevator that descends into the garage."

"Handy," Thack drawled.

Aubrey merely stared in amazement as Zack slid back the door to reveal a small lift, complete with telephone mounted on the wall.

"Right," Zack concurred with Thack's observation. "As you will see, the garage is the only section of the lower level that's attached to the upper levels. The elevator runs from the garage up to my workroom on the floor above this one."

A devilish grin revealed his white teeth as he ushered them into the cubicle. "The waiter from the restaurant used the lift to bring our lunch up; the dishes will go down the same way."

Thack laughed out loud. "You know, I was so busy talking, I never noticed where the guy came from."

Aubrey hadn't noticed, either; the waiter had appeared to materialize out of nowhere. Then another thought struck. "You said you eat breakfast in the restaurant every morning," she said to Zack. "Is this how you get there?" she moved her hand to indicate the lift.

"Occasionally." Zack nodded. "But as a rule, I use the outside stairs. I only use the elevator when I return late at night."

The lift came to a stop, and after Zack slid the door open, they stepped onto the cement floor of the three-car garage. The Jaguar was parked in one of the stalls; the other two were empty.

"You can drive your vehicle into one of the stalls, Thack." Leading the way, Zack headed for the front of the garage. He touched a button on the wall as he passed, and the wide garage door slid up and along the ceiling. They walked outside onto a paved driveway that led onto the complex's parking area and the highway beyond.

"Damned convenient," Thack said, glancing around with interest. "You've got a smart outfit here, Zack."

"And the location is absolutely magnificent," Barbara complimented. "Did you choose it for inspiration for your work?"

Painfully reminded of her husband's search for "artistic inspiration," Aubrey studied Zack as she waited for his answer.

"Inspiration?" Zack frowned, then shook his head. "No. I decided on this location simply because I liked it more than any of the other properties I looked at." He smiled gently at Barbara. "The inspiration for my work comes from in here—" he tapped his temple with a forefinger "—it always has."

Suddenly Aubrey felt as if she couldn't breathe properly. With Zack's quiet statement ringing in her ears, she stepped away from the group. "I must go." Forcing a smile, she glanced at Thack and Barbara. "It was a pleasure to meet you, and I hope—"

"Hey! Wait a minute," Zack interrupted. "You sound like you're not expecting to see Thack and Barbara again."

Although that had been Aubrey's intention, she couldn't just blurt it out. "Well, you and Thack have a lot of catching up to do. I—I don't want to intrude," she finished lamely.

"Intrude? Aubrey!" Zack started toward her, then, realizing he had an interested audience, hesitated, his body taut with frustration. "Look, you go do whatever it is you have to do. I'll get Thack and Barbara settled in and then . . ." Zack's voice trailed away as he realized he was not exactly sounding like an eager host.

As if tuned in to Zack's thought process, Thack read his brother's expression perfectly. "Don't concern yourself about us," he told Zack easily. "We were looking forward to poking through the gallery, anyway."

Zack was feeling decidedly pressured. Although part of him urgently wanted to go back to the motel with Aubrey, another part needed to stay to get better acquainted with the brother he hadn't seen in thirty years. Zack raked his mind for a solution that would appease both sides, and suggested the first idea that occurred to him. He fervently hoped Aubrey would agree.

"Would you object to another tour of the gallery?" Zack asked Aubrey, clasping her hand as if afraid she'd suddenly bolt away from him.

"Object!" Aubrey exclaimed on a small laugh. "I'd love it, but—"

"Okay," Zack cut in, positive he didn't want to hear her continue. "You go do what you have to do, and I'll come get you, oh, about seven. The four of us can have dinner together in the restaurant. The gallery will be closed by the time we've finished eating." Zack paused to smile at her. "Then you and I will give Thack and Barbara a private tour of the place." He performed his eyebrow trick for her. "Yes?"

Aubrey was not unaware of how he'd linked their names in the same way he'd coupled Barbara and Thack's. She was also not immune to his coaxing charm. She knew she should refuse; she knew she would agree. Still, she tried to hold out against his lure.

"Yes?" Zack repeated in a whisper.

"Yes." Aubrey caved in with a sigh. "If that suits Thack and Barbara."

"Suits me fine," Thack said laconically.

"And me." Barbara laughed. "As a matter of fact, I was considering a nap. We left the hotel in San Francisco early this morning."

"It's settled, then." Zack gently squeezed Aubrey's hand. "I'll walk to the motel with you."

"Don't be silly." Slipping her hand from his, Aubrey took a step back. "I'm perfectly capable of crossing the road by myself. You help Thack with the bags." She started moving down the driveway, then called back, "I'll see you all at seven."

Zack watched Aubrey until he lost sight of her where the driveway curved onto the highway, then he glanced around at his guests. "Okay," he said briskly. "Let's get you two settled in. Then I think *I'll* grab a nap."

Zack couldn't sleep, but then he really hadn't expected to. Sprawled in the chair before the cold fireplace, he stared sightlessly into the pile of gray ashes. Inside his mind, Zack was reliving the tension and sensual excitement of the night before and, even though the ashes in the fireplace were cold, his body was heating rapidly.

Shifting uncomfortably, Zack combed his fingers through his hair. Damn, he ached to be with Aubrey now, alone and naked. He wanted to touch her, taste her, bury himself in her, feel the thrill of her tight warmth drawing him deeper and yet deeper into her velvety heat.

Exhaling harshly, Zack absently massaged the taut muscles at the back of his neck and smiled wryly at his body's response to his erotic thoughts. Never had he wanted a woman as much, or as painfully, as he wanted Aubrey.

But how did he want her? Zack answered the mental question without hesitation. He wanted her tomorrow morning, at his breakfast table. He wanted her forever.

Springing out of the chair, Zack paced the bedroom distractedly. Satisfying his wants would not be easy, even the immediate, physical want now that his brother was in residence.

Talk about timing! Shaking his head, Zack veered toward the window that faced onto the courtyard. The late afternoon tourist traffic was heavy; Zack barely noticed. He was wrestling with the problem of a brother and sister-in-law in the apartment and a lover in a motel room across the road.

Fate did have a penchant for playing funny little tricks at times, Zack mused, unamused. After nearly thirty years of longing to be reunited with his twin, why had Fate decided to lead Thackery to his door at this crucial period? And a Thackery head over heels in love, at that.

Thackery and Barbara. Zack smiled softly. Lord! Witnessing the feelings the couple had for each other was almost embarrassing. Thack had retired from the Rangers for Barbara, and Barbara had tossed aside a lucrative career for Thack.

The consideration sparked speculation in Zack's mind. Was he so much in love he'd willingly turn his back on sculpting for Aubrey? He didn't need the money his work brought; he'd accumulated more than enough to live in comfort the rest of his life. Did he need the work? Zack reflected. He had always thought he did. Yet since meeting Aubrey, he'd barely given a thought to the incomplete project on his workbench.

Umm, interesting. Frowning in thought, Zack returned to pacing the room. How far he was willing to go wasn't his major consideration. Zack *knew* he was irrevocably in love. At this point in time, Aubrey was the big question mark. What was Aubrey feeling now? The anger and fear that he'd experienced while watching her sleep in the early hours of the morning was back, clawing at his emotions.

Had Aubrey used him to compensate for her emotional emptiness? Or did she feel an attraction stronger than the physical? Zack stopped pacing to stare bleakly into nothingness. Had he represented a convenience, necessity or compulsion? Zack shook his head. He had no answers. He needed to talk to her.

But if she loved, would Aubrey be willing to turn her back on her career? The answer to that question was academic as far as Zack was concerned. He personally didn't give a rip if she pursued a career or not. The tormenting question for Zack was, would she be able to give up the past and the memories that continued to haunt her?

Suddenly bored with the confining four walls of his bedroom, and the unanswerable questions, Zack strode from the room in search of liquid fortification—in the form of a stiff shot of Scotch. On entering the kitchen, he discovered Thack examining the contents of his liquor cabinet.

"I hope you don't mind?" Thack raised an eyebrow at Zack as he turned from the cabinet, Chivas Regal in hand.

"Not at all—I told you to make yourself at home." A wry smile tugged at Zack's lips. "You know, I came looking for a drink myself. Maybe there's something to this theory of twins thinking alike."

"Could be." Thack slanted a narrow-eyed glance at him. "It seems we share other things, too." Pouring the whiskey into glasses, Thack handed one to Zack, then stared at him challengingly over the rim while he sipped from his glass.

Zack knew that Thack was leading to a specific point. Watching his brother steadily, he tasted his drink before replying. "Really? Like what?"

"When we fall in love, we fall hard."

Zack laughed softly. "Obvious as all that, is it?"

"I recognize the symptoms, since I suffer from the same malady," Thack drawled. "She is beautiful," he added sincerely.

Zack took another deep swallow from the glass, exhaling deeply as the liquor hit the back of his throat. "She is that," he agreed. "And you're right, I've got a bad case of that particular malady.''

"And Aubrey?" Thack probed. "Has she got a bad case, too?''

"Damned if I know," Zack admitted. "I haven't the vaguest idea what Aubrey's feeling.''

Eight

Aubrey was feeling an overwhelming urge to run. Stripped down to panties and bra, the open ends of a short cotton robe flapping against her thighs, she paced the width of the room in small, stiff-legged steps.

She had to get away from Zack, she *had* to get away. Going absolutely still, Aubrey trembled with the shudder that ripped through her slender body. Breathing deeply, she fought back the tide of panic rising in her.

Inspiration.

The word slammed into her consciousness. Aubrey winced as an image rose of Zack, gently tapping his temple with his forefinger.

"The inspiration for my work comes from in here—it always has."

A strangled sob lodged in Aubrey's throat, then whispered through her quivering lips in a soft protest against the flood of memories.

Clearly, too clearly, she could see Keith, his thin face bright with animation as he scampered over the deck of the sailboat his parents had moments before purchased for him. Claudia and Ralph Mason had happily written out the check for the sleek vessel to give their son the means to go sailing to the South Seas in search of inspiration for his art. Of course, Keith never had found the elusive motivation.

Aubrey could understand and forgive the Masons' indulgence of their only child. What she could not forgive was the role she'd played in the continued pampering of a full-grown man.

Would the scenario have read differently if she'd refused to tolerate Keith's childishness? Would she now, today, be back in Philadelphia, a marginally contented wife of a marginally successful painter or illustrator?

Aubrey doubted it. Yet eroding that doubt was the faint possibility that if she'd stood firm against Keith's willfulness, her daughter might still be alive.

Aubrey stood condemned before the faint glimmer of possibility. She was convinced the sentence was for life; she had only served three years of it.

Inspiration—how Aubrey hated that word.

The tremor in her body subsided as the memories receded. Feeling caged, Aubrey resumed the restless pacing, the urge to run washing over her again.

Four days remained of her hiatus. Today was Wednesday. Aubrey had an appointment to meet with the group for rehearsal in Tahoe on Monday morning.

Zack was beginning to unnerve her; Monday seemed a lifetime away.

The thought of Zack sent her gaze to the digital clock in the TV on the dresser. He had told her he'd come for her at seven. It was now six-fifteen.

A dizzying combination of fresh panic and sensual excitement rushed to Aubrey's head, more potent than the champagne she'd drunk with lunch. Images flashed inside her whirling mind. Images of Zack, flowing around her, over her, into her, his bronze body quivering in perfect unison with hers. Images of herself, crying his name, clasping him to her, surging hungrily to meet his advance.

Harmony. Ecstasy. Perfection.

Dear God, it wasn't possible. Shaking her head, Aubrey crossed her arms around her middle, as if afraid she'd shake herself apart. It wasn't possible to fall in love within twenty-four hours of meeting a man. It wasn't possible to experience soaring beauty in the physical expression of that love. Perfection was not possible!

A low moan shimmered on the still air in the room. Like a powerful magnet, Zack was drawing her to him, drawing her into his sphere, even to the point of involving her in his reunion with his brother.

And it was no use. The cry that broke from Aubrey's throat shattered the fragile hold on the tears gathering in her eyes.

It was no use! She was empty. There was no emotional gift that she could offer—only the depth of her despair.

Then why did the thought of Zack hurt her so much?

Denying the pain, Aubrey jumped to her feet. Dashing the tears from her cheeks impatiently, she tore the thin robe from her trembling body.

She had to run, put some distance between herself and Zack. But not now, not this evening. Tomorrow, Aubrey bargained with herself. She'd go tomorrow. But she had to have one more night with him. One more night. Deserving or not, she would allow herself one instant of glowing light to brighten the infinity of darkness stretching before her.

For whether it was possible or not, she did love him, and for a shining moment had touched perfection in the expression of that love.

Zack tapped lightly on the motel room door at exactly seven o'clock. Confident that her expression was free of the inner turmoil tearing her in conflicting directions, Aubrey swung the door open, a welcoming smile on her lips.

The very first thing Zack noticed were the haunting shadows in her eyes. Smiling gently, cursing silently, he caught her small hand with his and drew her from the room.

"You're so very beautiful." The murmur seemed to sigh from his lips as his gaze drank in the simplicity of her filmy dress in shades of pink and amethyst that gave a glow to her pale cheeks and enhanced the violet of her eyes.

"Thank you." Aubrey lowered her lashes as pleasure sent a rush of color to her cheeks.

"And am I not beautiful, also?" Zack expelled his breath softly as her lashes swept up to reveal startled but laughing eyes. His teasing remark had wrought the desired effect; the shadows in her eyes had been replaced by amusement.

"Well, let me see." Her expression mock serious, Aubrey stepped back to glide an encompassing gaze the length of his body and back. Attired casually, Zack still managed to look elegant in a blue on blue shirt, gray slacks and a sport jacket that fairly screamed "hand tailored." The overall effect on her senses was devastating. Aubrey was far beyond dissembling. "Yes," she whispered with a delicious shiver. "You are indeed beautiful, sir."

Every red blood cell in Zack's body heated to flash point, then surged through his veins. Every muscle in his body tautened, and his fingers tightened convulsively around her slender hand. For an instant, his reasoning faculties clouded by desire, Zack forgot where they were, where they were supposed to be in a few short minutes. All he knew was the throbbing in his body, the longing in his heart, the aching need to pull Aubrey into his arms— and never let her go.

Aubrey's bones were melting—she was certain they were melting; she could feel the burning heat softening them, leaving them weak and pliable.

Hold me. Kiss me. Touch me. Lost in the warmth of Zack's mesmerizing stare, Aubrey felt too weak to repeat aloud the pleas that beat in her head. Yet Zack sensed them just the same.

A flame leaped wildly in the brown depths of his eyes. Raising his arms unsteadily, he took a step toward her.

"I know and appreciate the feeling, bro, but I don't recommend a parking lot beside a public road." Thack's softly drawling voice snapped the invisible line of tension.

Zack's arm fell to his side as he stepped back, away from the temptation of Aubrey's sweetly parted lips. He inhaled slowly, then exhaled harshly before turning to face his brother.

"The Ranger to the rescue," Zack observed dryly. "And not a minute too soon."

"Ex-Ranger." Thack's tone was equally dry. "And since we'd decided that we're pretty much alike, I figured you didn't require an audience."

"You figured correctly," Zack agreed, tilting his head to slide a smoldering glance over Aubrey. "But at the moment, I wasn't thinking too clearly." A deprecating chuckle eased from his lips. "Hell, I wasn't thinking at all."

Embarrassed, flustered, Aubrey smoothed her palms over the gentle flare of her skirt and cleared her dry throat. "Wh-where is Barbara?" she asked raggedly.

Thack smiled, obviously understanding her need for the company of another woman. "Sipping on a very large frothy margarita," he replied, grinning. "And since it's already her second, I suggest we hightail it to the restaurant—" his grin widened "—or she'll be smashed before dinner."

"A very large frothy margarita sounds enticing." Smiling shyly, Aubrey started walking across the parking lot. Before the men fell into step with her, she muttered, "So does getting smashed."

Though Aubrey did indulge in the former, she didn't attain the latter. The conversation was lively throughout dinner. Once Barbara and Thack learned that Aubrey was a professional singer, they kept her too busy answering questions to reflect on the brief but intense scene between her and Zack in the parking lot.

"I gather, since you mentioned leaving San Francisco this morning, that you've been to see mother's lawyer." Zack dropped the question into the silence that had settled comfortably over the table while they lingered with liqueurs and coffee.

"Right." Thack's expression grew somber. "It was generous of... ah, mother, to remember me in her will. But it really wasn't necessary." A smile twitched the corners of his lips. "I have no use for an interest in a house in Palm Springs."

"Bitterness, Thack?" Zack probed understandingly.

"No." Thack shook his head sharply. "At one time, maybe, but..." He hesitated, glancing lovingly at Barbara. "I have everything I need now."

Zack shrugged. "So you can bring that everything to the coast for a vacation every so often." A teasing grin played on his lips. "And later even a passel of everythings. Hell, there's plenty of space; the house has fourteen rooms." He nodded at Barbara's surprised look. "I seldom go there anymore, and I'm positive Kit won't mind the company."

"Kit?" Thack frowned.

For an instant, Zack looked like he'd been struck speechless, then he softly exclaimed, "Ho-ly hell! Kit! She'll *kill* me!"

Thack glanced sharply at Aubrey then back to Zack, his expression baffled. "So okay. Who is this Kit, and why is she going to kill you?"

"My sister. Your sister." Zack raked a hand through his neatly brushed hair. "Our half sister!"

Thack went absolutely still for a second, then he leaned across the table to speak with quiet urgency. "I have a sister—a half sister named Kit?"

"Oh, Thack." The depth of feeling in Barbara's soft voice reflected the compassion welling in Aubrey. Blindly Thack groped for his wife's hand, while his gaze remained pinned on his brother.

"Yes," Zack said gently. "We have a half sister named Kit. Well, Kathryn legally, but we've never called her anything but Kit." Amusement sparked his eyes. "And she's going to kill me for not calling her the minute you arrived. She's been pestering me to contact you for years."

"Really? Why?" Thack still looked stunned.

His smile soft, Zack reached across the table to grasp Thack's tense hand, and in a lowered tone offered his brother the gift of family. "There are several reasons. For one, she has been dying to meet you for as long as I can remember. For another, our Kit is greedy. She wants *both* her brothers at her beck and call."

"A sister. Kit," Thack whispered in wonderment. Then, with a grin spreading over his handsome face, he turned to his wife. "Do you hear that, honey? We have a sister!" Without waiting for a response from his misty-eyed wife, he swung back to Zack. "When can I meet her? How old is she? Is she married or anything? Where is she now—in Palm Springs?"

Though Aubrey couldn't see Zack's expression through the mist of tears filling her eyes, she heard his burst of laughter.

"Hey, Thack, one question at a time, please." His laughter subsiding, Zack released his grip on Thack's hand and sat back in his chair. "Kit is twenty-five years old. She is not married—or anything." Zack frowned, thinking of Logan McKittrick. "At least, I don't know of anything," he qualified. "And no, Kit is not in Palm Springs now. She's in Nevada, running and attempting to sell the small gambling casino her father, Bruce Aimsley, left her when he died."

"Her father," Thack murmured contemplatively. "What was your stepfather like?"

The coffee cups were refilled and emptied again while Zack filled his brother in on the stepfather one of them had loved and the other had never known. It was going on ten o'clock when Zack finally answered the last of Thack's questions.

"When can we meet Kit?"

"I can introduce you by phone tomorrow morning," Zack offered. "Maybe you can talk her out of taking a strip off my hide. As to meeting her in person, well, you two could drive to Tahoe, unless Kit decides to immediately jump into her car and come here." His smile suggested that they shouldn't be surprised at anything from Kit. "Let's play it by ear when I call her."

"Good enough," Thack agreed, pushing back his chair. "And now we'd appreciate that tour you mentioned this afternoon."

Bidding good-night to the waiters and waitresses in the room, they left the restaurant and strolled across the flood-lit courtyard. As they approached the statue, Barbara gasped aloud at the beauty of the kneeling woman.

"I had read about this particular statue," she commented, moving closer to the gleaming copper sculpture. "In fact, I have a... friend who tried to buy it," Barbara added, slanting a glance at her husband.

"Vanzant," Thack muttered, his eyes narrowing at the thought of his wife's former lover.

"I've heard of him." Zack stared at his brother speculatively. "Big business. High powered. Lots of money."

"That's the one," Thack drawled easily, removing all doubt about his own confidence and his wife's faithfulness.

"I turned his offer down flat." Zack grinned in a secret, male way.

"Good." Thack returned the grin as he moved to examine the statue more closely. After circling the large piece, he stared at Aubrey. "You were the model for this?" He couched it more as a statement than a question.

"No." Aubrey felt an odd tingle skip down her spine.

"Could've fooled me." Thack shifted his gaze from Aubrey to the statue then back again. "Damned uncanny resemblance."

Aubrey watched as Thack grasped Barbara's hand to guide her down the path to the gallery, then she turned to gaze helplessly at Zack.

"Do you think I look like her?" Knowing how deeply he felt about the kneeling woman, Aubrey held her breath as she waited for his reply.

"Yes, remarkably like her," Zack admitted, moving to stand very close to her. "Now I'll never let her go," he murmured, his gaze capturing hers.

What was Zack trying to tell her? Aubrey wondered. A fluttery sensation rose in her chest. Panic? Excitement? Suddenly she didn't want to know what he was trying to tell her. She couldn't let herself know. She had nothing to give—any man. Breaking the bone-melting hold of his gaze, she hurried after Thack and Barbara, as if seeking their protection.

Aubrey stayed by the other couple throughout the entire tour of the gallery, most of the time practically glued to Barbara, who revealed a surprising amount of knowledge about the art. They lingered the longest at the small grouping of Zack's work currently on display. The pieces were not very large; a few were actually tiny. The majority were figures cut from wood.

"Aren't you afraid of theft?" Barbara asked, her fingers stroking the likeness of a belligerent-looking bull.

Zack's shrug conveyed unconcern. "The security system is very sophisticated," he assured Barbara, smiling gently. "Besides which, if I worried over every piece, I'd never finish one of them. Life's full of risk. If we're afraid to take chances, we'll have to be satisfied to live in a world without beauty."

Philosophical. Aubrey added the word to her list of adjectives describing Zack as she tugged the filmy dress over her head. After leaving the gallery, she had declined Zack's suggestion of a nightcap, opting to play it safe and go back to her room. Though Zack had escorted her to the door, she had evaded any physical move he might have made by having her key ready and slipping into the room with a soft "Good night."

"Aubrey?"

Zack's soft, questioning call still rang in her head, as did the echo of her own voice, firm, decisive, slightly raised to reach his ears through the solid wood barrier.

"I'll talk to you in the morning. Good night, Zack."

Now, contrarily, Aubrey was suffering pangs of regret. She was leaving early in the morning and had already requested a wake-up call for six-thirty. It was unlikely that she would ever see Zack again. There would be no morning for her and Zackery Sharp. She should have stolen a moment to lose herself in his arms.

Sighing dejectedly, Aubrey pulled a pin-striped, baseball-styled nightshirt on and crawled between the cold, unwelcoming sheets.

She had been far from cold the night before, despite the absence of sleep attire.

Memories sent warmth through Aubrey's body and she moved her legs with unconscious sensuality. The bed was wide and, except for the tiny island on which she was lying, clammy and cold.

With a sound quite like a whimper, Aubrey curled into a tight ball of misery. Was this to be her future from now on? she cried silently. Memories of her past haunting her by day, memories of one night of perfect union tormenting her at night?

Aubrey buried her face in the pillow to muffle a sob. God, life was a bitch.

"Are you trying to wear a path into the floor?"

Zack stopped midstride, head whipping around to the archway into the hall. Thack leaned indolently against the wall, brows raised in question as he observed his brother.

Zack had been pacing the living room, cursing himself for allowing Aubrey to slip away from him, ever since Thack and Barbara had retired to the guest room.

"I thought you were tired?" Zack ignored Thack's question to ask one of his own, then dropped like a stone onto a chair.

Pushing away from the wall, Thack sauntered to the long rattan sofa opposite Zack's chair and sat down. "She closed the door in your face, huh?"

Zack exhaled heavily. "Literally, figuratively and every other way," he replied moodily.

Thack studied his twin in silent commiseration for a moment, then, hesitantly, as if afraid of being rebuffed, he offered, "Want to talk about it?"

Zack also hesitated. Exchanging confidences of a personal nature had never been his style. But then, agonizing over a woman, any woman, had never been his style, either. Besides, talking to Thack would almost be like talking to his own reflection in the mirror.

While Zack teetered on the edge of uncertainty, Thack braced his legs, preparing to stand up. "Look," he said softly, "forget it. I can understand if you don't—"

"No!" Zack's head snapped up. "Don't go, Thack. Maybe it'll help if I bounce it off someone."

"Bounce away," Thack drawled expansively, settling back on the sofa and stretching out his long legs.

Briefly, concisely, Zack explained Aubrey's emotional conflict. His voice dropped to a low pitch when he got to the part about his own inner conflict. Had Aubrey made love to him to chase the shadows away, or had her response been because she had felt the same urgent attraction he did? A defeated smile twisted his lips as he summed up his feelings.

"I could handle the challenge of another man, or a career, but how do I fight the ghosts of the past?"

"With compassion. With understanding. With love." Thack regarded Zack steadily. "And using those weapons, by refusing to allow her to withdraw from the field of battle."

Zack raked his fingers through thick waves. "You're saying I was a fool to let her close the door in my face, right?"

"You got it."

"Yeah." Zack sat very still for a moment, then he sprang to his feet. "Yeah—dammit!" He was on the move, striding to the door to the outside stairs. "Don't wait up," he advised his brother as he reached for the knob.

"You're heading across the road apiece?" Thack asked with encouraging amusement.

"You got it," Zack tossed Thack's words back at him, along with a grin.

"Go get her, bro."

Zack was still smiling faintly over his brother's laconic advice when he raised a hand to rap softly against the door to Aubrey's motel room.

As light as the tap was, the sound penetrated through the light sleep Aubrey had drifted into. Disoriented, she jerked into a sitting position, wondering what had wakened her. When the tap came again, it was accompanied by a soft voice.

"Aubrey? It's Zack. Please open the door."

Aubrey moved her head slowly from side to side. Then she slid her feet to the floor and padded to the door. Staring at the painted panel, she fought a silent battle with herself.

Don't open it. Don't even answer him.

Just a few more minutes with him—five, three.

You'll only inflict deeper pain on yourself; don't open that door.

One tiny kiss, one moment of forgetfulness in his arms.

Do not open that door!
Go to hell!

Consigning her conscience to the flames, Aubrey twisted the lock and pulled the door open as far as the safety chain allowed.

"It's very late, Zack." Her ragged voice reflected the internal conflict. The determined set of his jaw caused her stomach to quake.

"Aubrey, sweetheart, release the chain and let me in."

"Zack...."

"Please, Aubrey." Zack's tone held more command than entreaty.

Her conscience shouted that she was doing the wrong thing all the while her trembling fingers fumbled with the chain. The instant the chain was disengaged, Zack pushed the door open, forcing her to retreat as he advanced into the room. His intent was clearly written in his expression, his measured step, his taut body.

"No." Aubrey's throat closed on the whisper as she backed into the room.

"Yes." Zack stalked her like a hunter.

"Zack, it's no use. Don't, please." Her voice wasn't too convincing, even to her own ears.

"I must." Zack's arms shot out to grasp her arms when her legs came in contact with the bed. Slowly he drew her to him. "I must," he repeated, sighing as her breasts brushed against his chest. "This is the only way I know to get through to you." His voice had dropped to a rough murmur. His warm breath moistened her temple as he bent over her. "You smell so good." His lips tasted the sensitive spot behind her ear, the tip of his tongue tested the satiny texture of her skin. His voice thickened to a groan. "Oh, God, Aubrey, I need you so much."

"Zack." What Aubrey had meant as a protest came out as a sigh of surrender. Flattening her palms on his chest, she turned her mouth to meet his. The inner battle resumed.

Send him away. This is not fair to him.

Just this one more night, please, just tonight.

You have nothing left to give.

Except tonight.

It's wrong.

It's beautiful.

The war ended on a whimper as Aubrey parted her lips for Zack's seeking tongue. His kiss deepened, consuming her, setting her on fire. The voice of conscience became almost a wisp of smoke lost in the haze of sensuality blanketing her mind.

Shiveringly aware of his hands sliding her nightshirt up her body, Aubrey was unconscious of her own hands, busy at work on his shirt buttons. Awareness became the feel of chest hairs against her fingertips, her palms, her body. Awareness sharpened with the taste of him filling her mouth with his hungry tongue. Awareness intensified as he removed his clothes, then drew her hands to the heart of his fiery heat. Awareness became an exquisite pain as he lowered her to the bed and covered her body with his.

"We must talk."

Zack's husky voice infringed on Aubrey's awareness. Lifting her heavy eyelids, she stared into the face of passion.

"No. Not now." Aubrey nipped at his lower lip and moved her body enticingly, invitingly.

"Tomorrow," she murmured, stroking the cord at the side of his throat with the moist tip of her tongue.

"Oh, God, yes!" Zack wasn't certain whether he responded to her action or her promise.

Dipping his head, he caught her mouth with his. Then he thrust into her simultaneously with his tongue and body.

Sated, replete, contented, Aubrey curled more tightly against Zack's body and let the world begin to drift away. A soft smile curved her lips as his arms flexed, drawing her up and halfway over his chest. She was shivering on the edge of sleep when a thought flashed into her mind. With a groan, she pushed her drained body from his.

"Come back," Zack commanded sleepily.

"In a moment," she promised, reaching for the phone.

The desk clerk answered on the second ring.

"This is room twenty-seven," Aubrey mumbled. "Cancel my wake-up call."

Nine

"Aubrey, wake up."

Murmuring in her sleep, Aubrey snuggled closer to Zack's warm body.

"Sweetheart, can you hear me?" Zack's breath ruffled the hair on the top of her head.

"Umm." The sound she made could have been interpreted as either a yes or a no.

Half exasperated, half laughing, Zack expelled his breath on a sigh. "Aubrey, please wake up—just for a moment."

Aubrey's lashes fluttered, then, with obvious reluctance, she tilted her head to gaze up at him through sleep-clouded eyes. "What is it?" she asked fuzzily.

"Good morning." Zack smiled tenderly. "I'm leaving. I wanted to tell you I'm going back to the house. I didn't want you waking alone and wondering where I'd gone."

"What time is it?" Aubrey's voice cleared somewhat as she struggled out of her drowsy state.

"Seven-ten."

"Must you go?" The question slipped out before she was fully awake.

"Yes. I have houseguests, remember?" Stroking his fingertips along her jawline, Zack tipped her face up to meet his descending mouth. "I don't want to go," he sighed against her lips, "but I think I'd better."

Aubrey's mouth came awake faster than she had. Her lips parted to meld with his, her tongue teased the edge of his teeth.

"Ah, sweetheart, now I know I'd better go." Kissing her fast and hard, he drew away and rolled off the mattress. "If I don't get out of here now," he muttered, stepping into his slacks, "I probably won't make a move before noon."

Aubrey watched him solemnly as he finished dressing, her lashes lowered concealingly. When he was dressed, he leaned over the bed to kiss her again. Though she returned the kiss, she didn't try to prolong it.

"Breakfast?" Zack asked as he straightened.

"When?" Aubrey's lashes dropped lower.

"An hour? Two?" Zack arched an eyebrow.

Aubrey's lashes fluttered up as she slowly ran a devouring gaze over the length of his body. "Two," she whispered, her throat tightening around the deliberate lie; Aubrey planned to be long gone two hours from now.

Zack smiled indulgently. "Okay, sleepyhead, nine-fifteen in the restaurant." As if afraid he'd change his mind if he didn't go at once, he strode to the door and out of the room without looking back.

If Zack had given in to the urge to glance over his shoulder, he'd have seen the first tear that trickled down Aubrey's face.

Zack was whistling softly as he took the outside stairs two at a time, then entered the living room of the apartment. A smile tilted his lips at the call from the kitchen.

"Coffee's ready, Zack. If you can come down off cloud nine long enough to drink some."

Zack was grinning complacently when he strolled into the kitchen. "Barbara still asleep?"

Standing at the bar separating the kitchen from the dining room, a mug of steaming coffee cradled in his hands, Thack glanced over his twin's face before nodding in answer. "Is Aubrey, too?"

"Probably." Zack chuckled. "She was only half-awake when I left."

"Talked her into a stupor, did you?" Thack drawled dryly.

"Hardly." Zack laughed. "That is, we hardly did any talking at all . . . if you know what I mean."

Thack's expression spoke eloquently. "I didn't wash in on the last wave, bro." His lips twitched. "As a matter of fact, Barb and I had the same kind of late-night conversation." His dark eyes glowed with memory. "Best method of communication I know of."

Sipping the coffee he'd poured for himself, Zack grunted his agreement. "But," he qualified, "we're still going to have an in-depth discussion."

"I suppose." Thack sighed. "Falling in love does tend to complicate a man's life, doesn't it?"

His spirits soaring, Zack laughed again. "You got complications with Barbara, Thack?" he asked in a tone of disbelief.

"Not anymore." Thack grinned. "But things did get a little hairy for me before she decided to marry me and put me out of my misery. Hell, I couldn't sleep, I couldn't eat—" he shook his head "—I was a mess."

Zack looked at Thack skeptically; he had never met a man who seemed less likely to be rattled. So much for outward appearance, he mused, mentally shrugging. "Oh, by the way, I'm glad you mentioned eating. Aubrey said she'd join us in the restaurant in about two hours for breakfast. Okay?" Zack set his empty mug on the counter.

"Suits me." Pushing away from the bar, Thack walked to the coffee maker to refill his cup. "If Barb's not up in an hour I'll go tilt the bed."

"And I'm going to call Kit," Zack declared, reaching for the kitchen wall phone.

"Are you sure it's not too early?"

"Too early?" Zack grimaced. "It's too late, if you know what I mean." Sighing softly, he punched in the long-distance number. "She's going to give me royal hell," he muttered as Thack grinned.

Replacing the receiver a few minutes later, Zack frowned at Thack. "She isn't there. I spoke to the casino manager. He said she left a message that she'd be gone for a few days." A slow smile curved his lips into a devilish grin. "I'm off the hook, at least for a while."

Thack's eyes narrowed in contemplation. "You make Kit sound like a holy terror," he observed musingly.

"She can be." Zack laughed, turning for the hall and his bedroom. "And a tormentor, and a nag, and—" he paused at the doorway "—the most terrific, most understanding, most supportive friend in the world." He laughed again at the stunned expression on Thack's face. "Now, I'm for the shower."

Standing under the hot spray, Zack's body shivered as he relived the thrill of making love with Aubrey. Lord, they were so good together, he mused, absently soaping his tingling skin. And he felt positive they could be good together in all the ways that count between a man and woman... if only he could convince *her* of that. Determination turned his eyes to deep brown; he would convince Aubrey—one way or another.

Zack walked out of his bedroom thirty minutes later and grinned as he noticed the similarity in the clothes he and Thack were wearing. His choice of attire had not been deliberate—in fact, he hadn't really noted Thack's choice of clothes while they'd talked over coffee. Yet they had both chosen casual dress jeans, pullover sport shirts and brushed suede desert boots.

His back to the living room, Thack was standing at the window staring at the dark rain clouds swiftly approaching the coast. "It's gonna rain again," he observed blandly.

Zack halted abruptly at the archway into the room, his brows drawing together as he wondered how in the world his brother had detected his light tread. He was about to question Thack when the sound of running footsteps on the outside stairs distracted him. *Aubrey?* Even as the thought came to mind, the door flew open and his sister burst into the room.

"Zack! You've got to talk to that...that *boneheaded* Logan! He's...he's..." Kit's voice faltered as she stared at Thack.

Unobserved from his position at the archway, Zack smiled as he watched Kit's expression change to frowning confusion.

"When did you shave your beard and grow the mustache?" she demanded, striding across to Thack, who was eyeing her with interest. Halfway into the room she spied Zack. Kit's shoulder-length, silvery-blond hair was sent flying as she whipped her head back and forth from one man to the other. When her gaze settled again on Thack, her blue eyes widened and her lovely face bloomed with an expression of delight.

"Thackery!" As Kit shouted his name, she launched her tall body the rest of the way into the room and against his broad chest.

While his arms automatically closed around Kit's slim form, Thack gazed at Zack over her shining head. The emotions chasing each other across Thack's face brought a tightness to Zack's throat. To Zack, Thack looked exactly like a man who'd been given a priceless gift. Unable to resist the emotional tug, Zack joined them to form a triple hug-fest.

Questions. Laughter. Answers. Laughter. The air in the room vibrated with the joyous sounds of family, united at last. When Barbara wandered into the room, she was immediately swept into the circle of happy warmth.

"Hey, hold it!" Zack's raised voice brought the first bit of quiet in over an hour. "We've got to go; it's after nine."

"Go where?" Barbara and Kit spoke in unison, then smiled at each other.

"To the restaurant." Zack flung over his shoulder as he strode to the door.

"But..." Barbara began.

"Come along, ladies," Thack invited, draping an arm over their shoulders and urging them after Zack. "I'll explain along the way."

"She must have gone back to sleep," Zack said a half an hour later when Aubrey had not yet appeared. Noting Thack's conspiratorial look, he hid a grin as he got to his feet. "You might as well go ahead and order. I'm going to ring her room."

The conversation ceased when Zack returned to the table. His expression grim, Zack glanced directly at his brother.

"She's gone. She checked out of the motel a little after seven-thirty." Though Zack's voice was calm, inside he was a churning mass of hurt and anger and confusion.

Barbara and Kit stared at him in mute sympathy.

"Do you have any idea where she might have gone?" Thack queried softly.

"Yeah." Zack nodded. "To Tahoe."

"I just came from there!" Kit exclaimed.

"Ironic, isn't it?" Zack's smile held little humor.

A tense silence settled around the table. Then the quiet was shattered by a steely voice.

"Go after her."

As the advice was an echo of his own decision, Zack smiled wryly at his twin. "My thought exactly," he murmured. Then, cocking a brow, he added, "You know, Thack, this affinity we share is becoming damned eerie."

"But interesting," Thack commented. As Zack hesitated, he went on, "And don't worry about Kit. We'll use this time to get acquainted."

As Zack turned to leave the restaurant, Kit called after him.

"And if you happen to run into Logan, give him a punch for me!"

Shaking his head at his sister's not altogether teasing request, Zack bounded up the outside stairs.

By the time she handed the car keys to the doorman at the casino hotel in Tahoe, Aubrey felt physically and emotionally drained. Keeping her small frame erect by sheer willpower, she smiled wanly at the desk clerk while she checked into the hotel. Less than fifteen minutes later, Aubrey shut the door behind the bellhop and sank wearily into the solitary chair in the room.

Though bright and comfortable, the single room in no way resembled the hotel's more opulently decorated rooms that overlooked the breathtaking view of Lake Tahoe.

The room suited Aubrey. She wasn't looking for a view—she was looking for a hole to crawl into, or the equivalent thereof. Shoulders drooping with fatigue, she rested her head on the back of the chair, giving in to her exhaustion and despair.

Last night had been an error, Aubrey acknowledged, an error she would pay for throughout the rest of her life. In retrospect, she knew her biggest mistake had been in disengaging the security chain at Zack's request. The instant the door was no longer barred, her options had been eliminated; there was no way Aubrey could have refused him—or herself.

From the moment she'd opened her eyes that morning, Aubrey had accepted her share of responsibility for causing the situation she was now in. She also acknowledged that she must accept the consequences.

Watching Zack walk out of that motel room had been the most difficult thing Aubrey had ever had to do; stifling the outcry for him to stay had been the second hardest. Yet she had stifled the cry, as she had stemmed the flow of tears that scalded her cheeks.

Positive she was doing the right, the only, thing possible, Aubrey had flung herself into the task of dressing and tossing her belongings into her suitcase, while averting her eyes from the bed...on which she had so thoroughly lost all sense of self.

Closing her mind to memory, Aubrey had abandoned the room less than twenty minutes after Zack and had driven her rental car away from the motel. Except for the necessity of filling the gas tank, she had not stopped once—not for food or rest.

Now, locked inside her desperately sought sanctuary, Aubrey closed her eyes in defeat against the rush of memories that flooded her mind, and the flow of tears that washed her pale face.

Having her meals delivered to her room, Aubrey closeted herself for the entire three days remaining of her hiatus. By the time she ended her self-imposed confinement and walked out of the small room, Aubrey's delicate spine was straight, her expression calm, her eyes clear and her step, though light, was strong with purpose. For, after three long days of ruthless self-analysis, Aubrey had put the past behind her. She was prepared to face the future . . . and whatever it held for her.

Zackery Sharp, on the other hand, was at the point of tearing the hotel apart.

Where the hell was she?

After four days of searching everywhere he could think of for a tiny, beautiful, violet-eyed woman, Zack was used to the question that pulsed in his mind with frustrating regularity. And by late afternoon of the fourth day, Zack was beginning to question his own sanity.

Was he mad to be running around like an idiot, poking his head into every restaurant, bar, nook and cranny he came across, and peering into every feminine face in search of a woman who obviously didn't wish to be found?

Did he, in fact, harbor masochistic tendencies?

Staring morosely into a glass of Scotch he really didn't want but was drinking, anyway, Zack mused on his own mental stability.

Lifting the glass, Zack contemplated the amber color of the liquid while he reviewed his actions from the time he'd rushed out of the complex's restaurant and away from his newly united family—all of whom apparently loved him, as Aubrey, also apparently, did not.

Why didn't he simply pack his bag, get into his car and go home? Zack didn't have to ponder that query; it was the one and only question he knew the answer to. The answer was in the form of a poster, displayed throughout the hotel, advertising the appearance of Aubrey and her group in the lounge off the casino floor.

Nothing short of a major earthquake could have dislodged Zack from the hotel until after he'd confronted Aubrey following her final performance that evening. Till then, all that was left for him to do was sit and wait . . . and drink.

Considering the number of hours until Aubrey's final performance, the odds of Zack drinking himself into a stupor by then were definitely in favor of the house. But mythical lady luck decided to perch on the bar stool next to Zack in the form of one very large, very disgruntled Logan McKittrick.

"Is Kathryn with you?" said the big rancher by way of an opening statement.

Grateful for the diversion, Zack lowered the glass to the bar and turned to face Kit's stepbrother, who was obviously angry. The only time Logan ever called Kit "Kathryn" was when he was angry with her.

Although Logan was at least three inches shorter than Zack, the man had an indomitable look about him, which was reinforced by the fury blazing from his emerald green eyes. One of Zack's white-gold eyebrows arched questioningly as he glanced over Logan's harshly delineated features.

"Hello, Logan," Zack said easily, not at all put off by the man's steady regard. "Can I buy you a drink?"

"Sure." Logan accepted as easily as Zack had offered. "You can also answer my question. Is she with you?"

"No." Raising his glass, Zack tilted it at Logan in a silent salute. "She's at my place in California."

Logan lifted his glass and took a large swallow an instant after the bartender set it in front of him. "So," he said on a roughly expelled breath, "if Kit's there, what are you doing here?" His eyes narrowed dangerously, and before Zack could reply, he went on, "Did she send you here to talk to me?"

Not intimidated by the powerfully built man, Zack laughed softly. "Actually, Kit requested that should I run into you, I should give you a punch from her." His humor somewhat restored, Zack watched as the tension drained from Logan's taut body.

"Vixen," Logan muttered.

"But our vixen," Zack inserted smoothly.

"Yeah." Logan's tight lips gave way to a smile, revealing startling white teeth that were not quite even. "So she ran home to big brother, did she?'' He cocked a full, auburn brow at Zack and brushed at a shock of red-brown hair that had fallen forward onto his forehead. His big hand hesitated, then raked back through his thick auburn mane.

''And found more than she expected.'' Zack chuckled. ''She came tearing into my apartment and immediately demanded I tell her when I'd shaved my beard.''

Logan's gaze darted to Zack's narrow beard, then back to his eyes. ''But you haven't shaved your beard,'' he said with a frown.

''That's right, I haven't,'' Zack agreed, then waited for Logan to figure it out. He didn't wait long.

''Thackery's there?'' At Zack's nod, Logan exclaimed softly, ''Damn, that's great!'' His brows drew together. ''Or isn't it so great?''

''It's great,'' Zack assured around a smile, then waited again for Logan to assess the situation. The wait was even shorter this time.

''Hmm,'' the rancher mused laconically, ''Kit's in California. Thackery's in California. And you're here in Tahoe.'' His smile was desert dry. ''It has got to be a woman.''

''Right on the money,'' Zack admitted, exhaling sharply.

"Ain't we men the lucky ones?" Logan observed wryly. "Any way I can help?"

Zack started to shake his head, then paused, his smile every bit as dry as Logan's had been. "Yeah, you can sit here and get smashed with me."

"That's the best offer I've had in months," Logan said, grinning grimly.

As they sipped their whiskies and talked desultorily about mundane matters, neither Zack nor Logan managed to achieve the state of being smashed. When they parted company, Logan extended his hand and offered words of encouragement.

"Good hunting," he murmured. As Zack turned away he added, "And when you get back to the coast, tell the brat I want to talk to her."

"Will do," Zack promised with a final wave.

Zack walked into the crowded lounge as the group's appearance was being announced. A moment later, Aubrey exploded onto the stage exactly as she had weeks before in San Francisco. His pulses throbbing to the beat of the music, Zack devoured her tiny, shimmering figure with his hungry gaze while she electrified the audience with her performance.

Ordering a drink he didn't touch, Zack sat mesmerized through the entire set—and the other two sets—and wandered through the crush of people in the casino during the breaks between.

At the close of the last set, Zack's chest tightened and his resolve strengthened when Aubrey's riveting voice cried out the lyrics to the love ballad she'd sung in San Francisco.

Drench me in showers of rainbows to wash away all my sorrows.
And in return I'll promise the sweetness of all my tomorrows.

As the last haunting bars vibrated through the hushed room, Zack pushed back his chair, determined to make the lyrics a reality. This time he knew better than to tip a waiter to deliver a note. He'd get to her, Zack vowed, if he had to fight his way through a dozen hotel security men.

Zack was about to shove open a door marked Employees Only when he felt a light tap on his shoulder. Frustrated and ready for a fight, he spun around—and looked down into the shadow-free violet eyes that tormented his sleep.

"Hi. Looking for me?" Aubrey smiled tentatively; Zack looked so harried, so pushed to the edge. He stared, glared at her for a long instant of silence. Without a word, he then grasped her arm and strode toward a bank of elevators a short distance down the passageway.

"Zack!" Aubrey's exclamation was ignored by the angry man. When they were inside the ascending lift, she tried to speak to him again; Zack silenced her with a slicing movement of his hand and a drilling stare from his narrowed eyes.

When the elevator came to a halt, Aubrey was practically dragged out of it and along the corridor to his room. She was breathing heavily by the time he shut the door, locking her inside the room with him. Then he turned on her.

"Where the hell have you been the past four days?" Zack demanded in a tone he was obviously trying to keep even.

"Here." Aubrey gulped air into her lungs before adding, "In the hotel."

"Here?" Zack repeated incredulously. "Dammit, Aubrey, I've been driving myself crazy running around this place looking for you!"

He was so very angry that he frightened her. Aubrey felt a shiver tingle down her spine. At the core of her fear was a spark of excitement. Did Zack, she prayed, care so much for her that he'd been enraged by his inability to find her? The spark of excitement spread to mingle explosively with the fear.

"I—I didn't want to be found, Zack," Aubrey said tremulously. Her admission seemed to snap the control he was striving to hang on to. Cursing harshly, he grasped her by the upper arms and hauled her roughly against his hard chest. Clasping her slight body to his with one arm, Zack caught her chin with his free hand, tilting her face up as he bent over her.

"Damn you," he growled against her parted lips. "Damn you for agreeing to meet me, then running off without a word." Zack's angrily expelled breath warmed her skin. "You've been hiding out, while *I've* been tearing around this hotel like a lovesick idiot!" His lips brushed hers, igniting an instantaneous fire of need. "Damn you, woman, because I'll be damned if I'll let you get away from me!"

The vow was groaned into her mouth as her lips were crushed by the force of his. Zack was not gentle with her. Bruising her tender lips with his devouring mouth, he raked her small form with hands made rough by need before pulling her up and into the hardness of his body.

Aubrey's response was not a frightened stillness but an inflamed wildness that spurred him on. Even as he tore his lips from hers, he pulled the clingy, miniskirted costume from her quivering flesh. Within minutes, Zack had torn the clothes off both their bodies. Then, his chest heaving as he gasped for breath, he gazed at her with passion-hot eyes.

Shaken, more sexually aroused than she'd ever been before in her life, Aubrey stood rigidly, waiting for his next move.

"You claim to be empty, dead inside." Purpose glowed from the depths of the eyes he raised to hers. "Yet you've displayed an amazing capacity for life each time I've been inside you." His lips thinned. "Is that what it takes, Aubrey?" he grated. "Do you need a man's life force inside you to feel alive?"

He was being deliberately crude, deliberately cruel. Yet instinctively Aubrey knew Zack was lashing out at her because of the pain searing him, not the anger.

"No answer? No denial?" Zack stepped to her, his body taut, hard, beautiful. "Good, because I intend filling the emptiness in the only way you respond to."

Zack raised his hands, but before he could again grasp her arms she stepped back, away from him. Standing proudly, her delicate spine straight, Aubrey lifted her head regally. Watching him closely, she saw surprise flicker in his eyes, excitement flush his cheeks as she smiled invitingly before turning to walk to the single, king-size bed. Her movements sensuous, Aubrey grasped the spread and bedclothes and casually tossed them to the foot of the bed. Then, her violet eyes smoky with desire, she held his riveted gaze as she slid onto the mattress and held out her arms to him.

"Fill me with your life force, Zack, please." Aubrey's voice was a whispered plea.

"Oh, God, Aubrey!" Zack's groan vibrated in the still air. Then he was on the bed with her, his mouth a brand, his tongue a flame, searing her lips, the vulnerable curve of her neck, the gentle curve of her small breasts.

Aubrey whimpered with pleasure as Zack's teeth delicately raked her aroused nipple and arched her back convulsively when his lips closed around her to suckle gently. Needing to touch him, she skimmed her hands over his shoulders and down his broad back. When Zack brought his mouth back to hers, murmuring encouragement even as he nipped at her lower lip, Aubrey guided her hands to the heat of him, testing his weight in her soft palms.

"Oh, my love, yes!" Zack moaned into her mouth. "Feel the life pulsing in me. Bring me to you to fill your emptiness."

"Zack!" Aubrey cried aloud as he thrust deeply into her. "Oh, Zack, yes!"

Ten

"**Y**ou can't solve anything by running away." Lying on his back beside Aubrey, Zack drew a deep breath and listened to his heartbeat return to normal. Though his voice was steady, Zack's mind still reeled.

"I know." Eyes closed, Aubrey savored the feeling of absolute contentment that was a direct result of their lovemaking.

The distant sound of her voice robbed Zack's satiated body of the boneless sensation he'd been enjoying. Stomach muscles clenching over the unease he felt uncurling inside, he shifted to his side, supporting his torso on his forearm while his other hand slid possessively over her abdomen.

"Aubrey," he murmured urgently, caressing her face with his anxious gaze, "you cannot survive in this continuing state of angst; you *must* let go of the past."

Drawn by the warmth of his body, Aubrey turned to him, her hand moving to rest on his slim hip.

"Zack, I—" she began hesitantly, as if gathering her thoughts.

"Sweetheart, let me help you." Afraid to hear what she might say and determined to make his plea first, Zack hurriedly cut her off. "Let me share the burden of your loss." His voice lowered to a ragged whisper. "Aubrey, I love you."

"Oh, Zack..."

"No, let me finish." Zack's intense tone cut off her words. "I'll give you all the time, all the understanding you need, if you'll only stay with me. I know you'll always have an empty spot in your heart for your daughter, but let me try to fill the rest of it. I'll give you another child—I'll give you a dozen babies, if it will help. Darling, I promise I'll do my utmost to fill you with life.''

''I want your babies, Zack,'' Aubrey inserted clearly when he paused for breath. In any other situation his expression might have amused her. Now she smiled softly.

''Aubrey, sweetheart, please tell me you're saying what I think I'm hearing.'' Zack's gaze pierced her as if searching for truth.

Aubrey brought her hand up from his hip to his tightly clenched jaw, then she slid her trembling fingers over his lips. ''Zack, I locked myself in my room for four days to do some serious soul-searching.'' His lips moved, but Aubrey pressed gently to bar the passage of his words. ''Now let *me* finish.'' Zack responded with a brief nod.

''When I ran away from the motel, I wasn't running away from you. I was running from the truth, from the realization that your image had replaced my daughter's in my mind and in my heart.'' Aubrey's voice wavered, almost as if the admission hurt her, but her tone gained strength as she continued. ''Zack, there will always be a part of me that belongs solely to my baby. I know that. But I also know that the way I've been living—or not living—since the accident will never bring my child back to me.

"Aubrey." Zack's soft tone vibrated with emotion. Releasing his light hold on her hip, he raised his hand, encircling her wrist with strong fingers. Gently, almost reverently, he kissed her fingertips. "Darling, I truly understand that a part of you will always belong to your daughter." He slid his lips to her palm. "But the rest of you can know the fullness of life."

"Zack." Aubrey sighed his name as his mouth caressed her palm.

"I know it's an inept comparison, but in a way, I spent thirty years of my life with an empty spot, too." Raising his head, Zack gazed into her eyes. "There were times that I longed, deeply, secretly for my brother. Times when I resented never knowing anything about him. Times when I simply missed the fun we might have had by not joining in sports together or double dating, or—" his lips twitched in amusement "—driving friends and teachers crazy with our identities." Zack's smile grew sad. "And even though I have Thack with me now, those years are gone and they can never be recaptured. While living through those years, love, there were times when I hurt badly. But I did live those years to the fullness of my capabilities.'' Bending, he brushed his lips over hers. ''You will have the hurtful times, too, love. But I will always be there for you. I love you, Aubrey.''

''I love you, Zack. I didn't want to, but I do. And, although I still think you deserve much better, I'll stay with you for as long as you want me.''

''I'll let you know the minute I grow tired of you.'' A choking laugh stuck in his throat. ''I don't expect it to last more than seventy or eighty years, at best.''

''Oh, Zack!'' Tears welled, then spilled over Aubrey's lids. ''I'll try to be everything you want,'' she cried softly. ''I love you so very much.''

Pulling her tightly to him, Zack closed his suspiciously bright eyes and buried his face in her silky hair. ''Don't cry, love. It will be all right, you'll see. We'll make it all right, as long as we're together.''

Clinging together, physically exhausted, but emotionally renewed, they finally drifted into sleep. Less than three hours later, the ringing of the phone shattered their slumber. Groggy and irritated, Zack reached for the receiver.

"Yes, what is it?"

"Trouble," Thack said succinctly. "I'm sorry I had to wake you, Zack, but I thought you should know that the rain has undermined the hillside above the gallery."

"What!" Zack was now wide awake, and sitting bolt upright.

"What is it?" Aubrey was also awake, frowning worriedly at him. "Who is it?"

"It's Thack," he replied distractedly. "Go on, Thack," he urged his brother.

"A section of the hillside has already broken loose and buried the garage and the gallery room next to it," Thack explained tersely. "It's only a matter of time before the rest of the hill goes. I'm afraid you're going to lose the entire gallery, Zack."

"The rest of the complex?" Zack asked tightly.

"There's no danger to the remainder of the structure, it's only the hillside directly behind and above the gallery that has been undermined by water."

"Damn!" Zack raked his fingers through his sleep-tousled waves. "Okay, Thack, I'm on my way. Thanks for minding the store for me."

"That's what families are for." Thack's tone said, Thanks for allowing me into the family.

As he replaced the receiver a sad, understanding smile briefly feathered Zack's lips, then they thinned into a straight line as he stood up wearily.

"I've got to get back," he said to Aubrey and went on to explain the situation at the complex.

"Not the gallery!" Aubrey exclaimed, scrambling off the bed.

Zack paused in the act of pulling on the slacks he'd tossed to the floor a few hours earlier. "Yes, the gallery." He sighed. "I probably can't do anything, but I want to be there just the same."

"I'm going with you." Scooping up her dress, she tugged it over her head.

"But what about your engagement here in the lounge?"

"I quit." Rolling her panty hose into a ball, Aubrey slid her bare feet into her spike-heeled sandals. Looking stunned, Zack just stared at her as she started for the door. "I have to change and pack. I'll meet you in the lobby in a few minutes."

"Aubrey!" Zack came out of his near trance as she reached for the doorknob. Crossing to her, he grasped her arm to turn her to him. "Darling, are you sure?"

"Yes." Raising up on her tiptoes, Aubrey brushed her lips over his. "The first thing I did last night after leaving my room was inform the group I was quitting. Our agent has already arranged for a replacement singer to finish this engagement." Easing back on her heels she smiled up at him sadly. "If you hadn't wanted me, I'd planned on going home to Philadelphia."

"You *are* going home, love," Zack murmured, bending to brush his lips over hers. "Your home is with me." Straightening, he spun away from her. "Now get a move on," he ordered thickly. "We've got to get out of here."

They were on the road less than an hour later, both quiet with their own fears and speculations about what they'd find when they arrived at the gallery.

Worn out, Aubrey found herself fighting the weight of her heavy eyelids after they'd been driving for two hours.

His frustrations and insecurities about Aubrey relieved, Zack was fully alert, adrenaline pumping into his system in preparation for whatever he had to face at home. The extra energy washed the exhaustion from his body. He slanted a glance at Aubrey as the first drops of rain splattered against the windshield, a tender smile softening his compressed lips.

"Don't fight it, love," he urged quietly. "Rest your head back and go to sleep."

Aubrey wanted to insist that she was fine, but it would have been an outright lie. Giving in to her fatigue, she settled her head against the headrest and closed her eyes. Within minutes she was lulled to sleep by the swish of the windshield wipers. It seemed like only seconds later that her eyes flew wide at the sound of Zack's low voice.

"We're home, sweetheart. Wake up."

Aubrey opened her eyes as Zack made the turn off the road onto the curving driveway that led to the complex's parking lot and the garage beyond. Driven before the wind, the rain slashed across the land in sheeting waves.

Aubrey couldn't see the gallery until Zack brought the car to a stop on the parking lot. Then, what she saw brought a gasp of dismay to her lips.

The garage and a corner of the gallery were crushed beneath a massive slide of earth and rocks. Streams of water ran over the glass roof of the remaining section of the gallery. For a moment, the occupants of the car were silent—shocked at the sight of the damage. Then Zack sighed heavily.

"Oh, darling, isn't there anything we can do to save it?" Aubrey cried, unable to tear her gaze away from the destruction.

"No, Thack was right. It's a total write-off." Turning to her, he noticed the tears sparkling on her inky lashes and decided action was called for. Releasing the door, he swung it open.

"Come on, love," he ordered gently. "We're going to get soaking wet, but there's no help for it. Let's make a dash for it." Springing from the car, he ran to get their cases out of the trunk. As he slammed the trunk lid closed, Aubrey jumped from the passenger seat and raced toward the restaurant level of the complex. Zack was beside her before she'd taken three steps.

Even at a run, Aubrey could see the door to the gallery. Twisted and standing ajar, the door had been forced open when the dirt and debris of the hillside had fallen on the roof. Shuddering, she ran on, across the courtyard and through the high gate that led to the stairway to Zack's living quarters. The door to the apartment was swung open as she and Zack gained the top of the stairs.

"Don't stop, Aubrey," Zack commanded as she ran into the apartment. "Go into the bedroom and get out of those wet clothes." Zack stayed on her heels, calling out, "Thanks, Thack," as his twin slammed the door behind them.

"No sweat," Thack drawled, then called, "There'll be hot food and coffee waiting for you when you've changed."

"We need both. We didn't stop to eat," Zack informed him before he shut the bedroom door.

Shivering, Aubrey made a beeline for the bathroom. She'd dropped her sodden suede jacket and silky knit shirt to the floor by the time Zack stepped into the room—completely naked.

"Come on, love, get out of those wet things," he growled, his fingers tugging at the snap at the front of her jeans.

"You get the shower water regulated," Aubrey advised, brushing his hands away. "Lord, that rain's cold!"

The stinging hot spray from the shower soon chased the chills from Aubrey's body; Zack's caressing hands as he soaped her from head to toe induced an altogether different kind of shiver.

"Zackery, we can't!" Aubrey protested weakly as he grasped her body and pulled her against his heat. "They're waiting for us for lunch."

"Let them appease their hunger their way," Zack groaned, bracing himself to support her weight. "And I'll appease mine my way." Cradling her body, he slid inside her.

Aubrey had never made love in the shower before, with silky water cascading over her passion-flushed body. She found it the most erotic sensation imaginable, and didn't even notice when the water sluicing their bodies ran cool.

* * *

Thackery's broad grin welcomed the couple when Aubrey and Zack finally strolled hand in hand into the dining room.

"All warm and dry and—everything?" he queried in a heavy drawl.

"All warm and dry and—everything," Zack returned, grinning down at Aubrey's glowing face.

"Well, are you planning to introduce me," Kit chided, "or are you going to stand there all day, grinning like a love-smitten idiot?"

Startled, Aubrey glanced at the young woman and knew at once who she was; the family resemblance was strong, only in Kit it was all feminine. An impish smile tilted her lips and gleamed in her bright blue eyes. Aubrey liked her on sight. From Kit's open, friendly response, it soon became obvious the feeling was mutual.

While they ate the lunch Kit and Barbara had prepared, they discussed the gallery and the hopelessness of saving it.

"But surely you managed to save some of the pieces?" Aubrey asked anxiously.

Thack shook his head. "Too dangerous," he said flatly. "The rest of that hill could go any minute."

"But Zack's work's in there!" she exclaimed, staring reproachfully at Thack.

"Aubrey, I just found Thack," Zack said softly. "I wouldn't want to lose him to a mound of earth for the sake of a few pieces of sculpture."

Chastised, but unrepentant, Aubrey subsided, keeping her ideas to herself. Her mind swam with confusing thoughts. If the moment arose, she promised herself, she would steal down to the gallery and save his work. At least she'd then have something of value to offer him.

"Would you care to see it, Aubrey?" Zack's question drew her out of introspection.

"What?" Aubrey blinked. "I'm sorry, I wasn't listening."

"Nodded off again, did you?" Zack smiled indulgently. "I offered to show Thack and Barbara my workroom," he explained. "Do you want to come along?"

Aubrey was surprised to see that Thack and Barbara were walking into the living room. Kit was clearing the table. "Oh, ah, yes!" Sliding back her chair, Aubrey jerked to her feet; how long had she been woolgathering? she wondered. Then it struck her. This was the perfect opportunity! "Ah, you go ahead," she urged him. "I'll join you in a moment. I want to help Kit clean up."

"All right, but don't be long." A wry smile curved Zack's lips. "I don't like having you away from me."

Resolve hardened inside Aubrey as she watched Zack stride into the living room. All the adjectives she'd compiled for him swirled in her mind. Zack was so good, so very good. He deserved the best. Her own pride had lost her her child. Perhaps courage would gain her the right to this man's love.

"Aubrey, I can handle kitchen duty," Kit called from the sink. "Besides, I've seen the workroom. Go on and join them. I'll be up as soon as I've finished."

Aubrey was moving before Kit completed her last remark. The deep rumble of thunder could be heard as she hurried toward the door. She paused only a moment at the curving staircase leading to Zack's workroom, then she was through the door and running down the outside stairs.

A jagged finger of lightning speared through the greenish-black clouds as Aubrey fumbled with the latch in the gate that opened onto the courtyard. She barely noticed the storm. The memory thread that had connected storms and the ocean to the loss of her daughter had been broken. Aubrey was not now seeking the sea, but a building in danger of collapsing, thus inundating the beautiful creations of the person she loved most in the world.

As she dashed through the rain swept courtyard, Aubrey linked the two in her mind. She had lost her treasure, the one beautiful thing she'd created, the child of her body and heart. If it was humanly possible, she would save Zack's treasures—for, having been shaped by his hands, they were the creations of his body and heart, as well.

Meanwhile, Zack was becoming uneasy with the first crackle of lightning. Glancing at the stairs for a sign of Aubrey, he continued explaining to Thack about the tool he held in his hands. A shiver of dread shot through him when Kit called to him from the living room.

"Zack, Aubrey's gone. The door is standing wide open."

In four strides Zack was at the north wall, composed of glass from four feet above the floor. Positive he'd spot her, his gaze raked the path along the bluff. She wasn't there. As he turned away, he caught a flash of color through the window wall that faced onto the courtyard. Stepping closer, he saw Aubrey, her white blouse plastered to her body, running across the yard. Zack knew immediately where she was going.

"Jesus!" Tossing the tool onto the workbench, Zack turned and dashed for the stairs.

"What is it?" Thack demanded, right behind him.

"She's heading for the gallery!" Zack's voice was tight with fear.

"Jesus!" Thack's whisper echoed his brother's exclamation.

Hold just a little while longer, Zack silently begged the crumbling hillside as he clattered down the outside stairs.

Thunder rumbled overhead as side by side Zack and Thack raced across the courtyard, leaping over puddles and pieces of broken branches. Thack's arm snaked out to steady Zack when he skidded on a patch of pebbly mud on the path to the gallery. Both men were panting, as much from apprehension as exertion, when they reached the partially open door.

"Damn!" Zack groaned with frustration. "I'll never be able to squeeze through there." Drawing a breath, he bellowed, "Aubrey, come the hell out of there!"

There was no answer; all that could be heard was the rain against the glass roof and the terrifying rumble of earth shifting. Eyes widening, Zack glanced at Thack then, in unspoken accord, they both grasped the door and pulled. For a moment, an endless moment, the twisted door held, then shuddered as it scraped the ground, inching outward. The instant the opening was wide enough, Zack slipped inside.

His heart hammering in his chest, Zack moved to the middle room. Aubrey was over by the broken table on which his work had been displayed, digging through the rubble.

Zack wanted to shout to her to stop, but was afraid the noise would set the earth into motion, burying the two of them under its weight. Without a word he bent and scooped her into his arms. Whipping around he dashed for the door Thack was still holding open.

"Is she all right?" Thack asked, trotting beside Zack as he ran up the path.

"Other than being crazy, I think so," Zack replied, panting.

"Zack, I'm sorry," Aubrey sobbed. "I wanted so desperately to save it all. And all I could find was this." Opening her hand, she revealed the small, belligerent-looking bull.

"Dammit, Aubrey!" Zack snapped. "You could have—" The sound of his voice was drowned out by the mighty grumble of the earth as it went crashing down onto the gallery.

Then there was an awesome quiet. Even the hiss of the rain diminished as the storm moved toward the east. Aubrey's soft sobs filled the sudden stillness.

"Your dream. Oh, Zack your beautiful dream. It's gone."

"It was a building, Aubrey." Carrying her easily, Zack strode back to the stairs, mounting them slowly as he spoke soothingly. "A building can be replaced. You can't."

"But your work," she cried, burying her face in his sodden shirt. "Those pieces can't be duplicated, not even by you."

"But I can create others, love." Zack's arm tightened around her. "I can't create another Aubrey."

Leaving Thack to answer Kit's and Barbara's questions about Aubrey's condition, Zack went directly to his bedroom and stood under the shower with her for the second time that afternoon. This time he didn't make love to her.

After Aubrey was dry and dressed in one of Zack's T-shirts, he sat her on the bed, talking softly while he blow-dried her mass of tangled hair.

"I want you to marry me as soon as legally possible." The brush in his hands paused. "Will you?"

"Yes, Zack," Aubrey answered vaguely, growing extremely sleepy from the warmth stealing over her.

"And, until we can be married, I want you to stay here with me." The brush paused again. "Will you do that?"

"Yes, Zack." Aubrey's voice was muffled.

Bending over, Zack peered into her face, then decided to test to see if she was answering automatically or if she was aware of what she was agreeing to.

"That's good, because I think you need a full-time keeper."

"I do not." Aubrey's voice, though still unclear, was adamant. "I'm so sleepy, Zack."

"I know, love." Shutting off the dryer, he set it aside, then pulled the covers back invitingly. "Crawl in, sweetheart," he said softly.

"Crawl in with me," Aubrey pleaded, stretching out on the bed. "I'm lonely."

She turned to him as he slid onto the mattress beside her. Curling her arms around his neck, she burrowed into the warmth of his body. "I failed again," she whispered against his skin. "Oh, Zack, I wanted so badly to offer you something of value by saving your work, but I failed."

"Your life is all I need," Zack murmured into her scented hair. "Just love me, Aubrey, for when you love, you love deeply and wholeheartedly."

"I do love you, Zack. Much, much more than I do my own life. And now life is so very important to me."

Zack's body shuddered with the spasm of joy that washed through him. Aubrey was no longer empty.

Murmuring in her sleep, Aubrey reached for the warmth of Zack's body. She woke when all her hands touched were the cool sheets.

"Zack?"

"Here, love." Standing at the window, Zack turned to hold out his hand to her. "Come here, Aubrey. Look."

Slipping off the bed, Aubrey padded to stand beside him, following the direction of his hand as he gestured to the courtyard. The sky was a brilliant sapphire blue, shot through with streaks of vermilion. Trailing his line of vision, Aubrey gazed at the statue in the courtyard. Rain washed, the kneeling woman gleamed copper red in the setting sun's rays.

"She's beautiful," Aubrey whispered.

"I would never sell her, never," Zack said softly. "And now I know why. When I made her, I made her in the image I carried in my heart. The image of the woman I was searching for. The woman I loved. She's you, Aubrey. And I'll no more let you go than I would her."

Arms entwined, they watched the copper woman kneeling in the warmth of the sun.

* * * * *

Take 3 of "The Best of the Best™" Novels FREE

Plus get a FREE surprise gift!

Special Limited-time Offer

Mail to The Best of the Best™

P. O. Box 609
Fort Erie, Ontario
L2A 5X3

YES! Please send me 3 free novels and my free surprise gift. Then send me 3 of "The Best of the Best™" novels each month. I'll receive the best books by the world's hottest romance authors. Bill me at the low price of $3.99 each—plus 25¢ delivery and GST*. That's the complete price and compared to the cover prices of $4.50 each—quite a bargain! I understand that accepting the books and gift places me under no obligation ever to buy any books. I can always return a shipment and cancel at any time. Even if I never buy another book from Harlequin, the 3 free books and the surprise gift are mine to keep forever.

383 BPA AQMQ

Name	(PLEASE PRINT)	
Address		Apt. No.
City	Province	Postal Code

This offer is limited to one order per household and not valid to current subscribers.
*Terms and prices are subject to change without notice. All orders subject to approval.
Canadian residents will be charged applicable provincial taxes and GST.

CBOB-94   ©1990 Harlequin Enterprises Limited

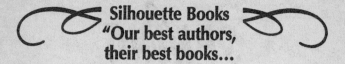

Silhouette Books
"Our best authors, their best books...

DIANA PALMER
Soldier of Fortune in February

ELIZABETH LOWELL
Dark Fire in February

JOAN HOHL
California Copper in March

LINDA HOWARD
An Independent Wife in April

HEATHER GRAHAM POZZESSERE
Double Entendre in April

*When it comes to passion,
we wrote the book.*

Silhouette®
™

SPRING fancy '94

**They're sexy, single...
and about to get snagged!**

Passion is in full bloom as love catches
the fancy of three brash bachelors. You won't
want to miss these stories by three of
Silhouette's hottest authors:

**CAIT LONDON
DIXIE BROWNING
PEPPER ADAMS**

Spring fever is in the air this March—
and there's no avoiding it!

Only from ▼ *Silhouette*®

where passion lives.

The price of paradise...

New York Times **Bestselling Author**

previously published under
the pseudonym Erin St. Claire

TIGER PRINCE

Lost in paradise, they began a fantasy affair.

Through hot Jamaican days and steamy nights, Caren Blakemore and Derek Allen shared half-truths and careless passion...

But as reality came crashing in, Caren learned the price. And she was left with only one way out....

Available in April at your favorite retail outlet.

Only from

where passion lives

**Fifty red-blooded, white-hot, true-blue hunks
from every State in the Union!**

Look for MEN MADE IN AMERICA! Written by some
of our most poplar authors, these stories feature fifty of
the strongest, sexiest men, each from a different state in
the union!

Two titles available every other month at your favorite
retail outlet.

In March, look for:

TANGLED LIES by Anne Stuart (Hawaii)
ROGUE'S VALLEY by Kathleen Creighton (Idaho)

In May, look for:

LOVE BY PROXY by Diana Palmer (Illinois)
POSSIBLES by Lass Small (Indiana)

You won't be able to resist MEN MADE IN AMERICA!